FEMME TALES

Visit us at www.boldstrokesbooks.com

FEMME TALES

by

Anne Shade

2020

FEMME TALES
© 2020 By Anne Shade. All Rights Reserved.

ISBN 13: 978-1-63555-657-5

This Trade Paperback Original Is Published By
Bold Strokes Books, Inc.
P.O. Box 249
Valley Falls, NY 12185

First Edition: March 2020

Credits
Editor: Cindy Cresap
Production Design: Susan Ramundo
Cover Design By Tammy Seidick

Dedication

This book is dedicated to women who are not afraid
to follow their hearts and love freely and openly
and to the women who are still finding their way.

Femme Tales

Beast   9

Awaken   91

Stiletto   141

BEAST

Based on the Beauty and the Beast *fairy tale*

Ebony Trent pressed pause on the remote to her office stereo system with a sigh. She'd been listening to demos for the past hour and was tired of hearing the same thing from every wannabe thug who thought they could rap. Tired of hearing about "niggas," "bitches," and "hos" and having the word "fuck" jammed abrasively in her ears as they talked about their ghetto, money, drug- and alcohol-filled lifestyle. She knew for a fact that two of the most profanity-laden, women demoralizing demos were from a suburban White kid from Long Island and a prep school Black kid from Jersey. The sad thing about it was that they were good. Their flow was smooth, but they were trying too hard to be something they weren't because they thought it was the only way to make it. Ebony didn't understand why these young kids tried so hard to be ghetto when she'd done everything possible to get out of the ghetto.

Ebony Trent, formerly known as The Beast, had come a long way from the infamous Cabrini-Green in Chicago. At fifteen years old, she was left to raise her ten-year-old sister,

Sheree, alone when their mother decided that a life on the streets as a crack addict was more appealing than raising her two kids. With the help of Virginia "Mama" Ellis, an older neighbor who would watch over and feed them when their mother was too high to bother, Ebony was able to keep Social Services from finding out their mother left. She managed to stay in school, keep her grades up, work a steady part-time job as a grocery cashier, as well as any other minor work she could find, legal or otherwise, to keep them out of foster care and keep a roof over their heads and food in their mouth. It was a hard life and one that bred a lot of anger for Ebony. The only thing that kept her from following in her junkie mother's and grandmother's footsteps was Sheree.

Ebony saw potential in her sister and was determined to make sure that Sheree was given every opportunity for success that Ebony was denied. Ebony knew the only way to do that was to get her out of the projects and break the cycle that had already broken two generations of Trent women.

Music was Ebony's drug, ever since she was a little girl sitting on her father's lap listening to his vast record collection of everything from classical to rock and losing herself in a world filled with musical notes, harmonious melodies, and poetic verses. It was the world she'd shared with her father before he was killed and one she frequently escaped to since his death. She wrote her own music, created her own beats, and sang her own hooks; her lyrics were filled with the pain and hardship of her life. After her best friend talked Ebony into entering a local rap battle when she was sixteen years old, music became her way out of the ghetto.

She was nicknamed The Beast for the raw talent she showed in knocking her competitors down without uttering a profanity or using any of the derogatory phrases she hated being used so frequently by other rappers. She had surprised even herself by how quickly she rose through the ranks of underground rap. By the time she graduated high school, she was being sought after by several music labels, but it was a producer Cass Phillips from her favorite independent label, Pure Music, that offered her the deal that helped her and her sister escape from a life of struggle. The ink hadn't even dried on the contract before she packed up her sister and Mama Ellis and moved to New York without even a glance back. That was thirteen years ago.

Ebony glanced around her office, noticing the display shelf across from her desk that held trophies from the Underground Music Awards, BET Hip-Hop Awards, MTV Hip-Hop Awards, and her proudest, the Grammy she received for her last single on her retirement album, *Taming of the Beast*. Ebony hadn't disappointed Pure Music, giving them several chart topping solo albums and collaborations over the first five years before becoming a successful producer on their label for the last six years. Ebony had made sure that her good fortune was also her loved ones' good fortune.

She'd sent Sheree to the best private schools, and she was now a graduate student at New York University working on her master's in social work so that she could further her career as a substance abuse counselor. It wasn't a glorious job nor would she get rich from it, but Ebony couldn't have been more proud of her because she was doing something important. Mama Ellis was also still with them. If it hadn't been for her Ebony knew she'd probably be in jail or dead and Sheree would've ended up a product of the foster care system so Ebony made sure she didn't want for anything. They all lived in a brownstone in Harlem Ebony had purchased and renovated so that they could be together but still have their own space. Ebony felt there was nothing more she could ask for, yet there still seemed to be something missing in her life. A knock on her office door interrupted her thoughts.

"Come in," she called.

The door opened and Ebony's assistant, Dane, walked in, arms loaded down with shopping bags, followed by Mama Ellis.

"I ran into this beautiful little lady coming into the building on my way back from lunch." He set the bags near the sofa.

Ebony came from behind the desk and greeted Mama Ellis with a kiss on her smooth cheek. "This is a surprise. What are you doing here?"

"I came into town to do some shopping for the kids at the shelter and figured I'd drag you out to lunch since you probably haven't had anything since breakfast," Mama Ellis said knowingly.

"Thank you, Mrs. Ellis, 'cause Lord knows I try to get her to eat and she just waves me away." Dane grinned.

Ebony scowled at Dane who got the message and retreated without another word.

Mama Ellis patted Ebony's cheek affectionately. "You're so busy taking care of everybody else you forget to take care of yourself so somebody's got to do it."

"Between you, Sheree, and Dane I think I'm covered. So where would you like to go to lunch?"

"Why don't you pick the place but give me a minute to catch my breath before we go," Mama Ellis said.

She was a petite woman who was in much better physical health at sixty-five than she was at fifty because Ebony made sure she had the best healthcare available. Something she lacked when they lived in Chicago where she'd been suffering from Type 2 diabetes and high blood pressure. Ebony hadn't realized how bad it was until shortly after Mama Ellis's first doctor visit about a month after they arrived in New York when they were told that an infection in her right foot was so bad that if they had waited much longer to bring her in it would've needed to be amputated. Fortunately, they were able to clear the infection and put her on a regular regimen of insulin and blood pressure medication, both of which she was taking in lesser dosage after she started cooking healthier and, to Ebony's surprise, joined a seniors' exercise class.

"Are you all right, Mama Ellis?" she asked as she led her over to the seating area in her office.

"No need to go fussin' over me. I'm just a little tired, baby. They've been shorthanded at the shelter this week so I've been helping out more than usual. I'll be fine after a good night's sleep," she said tiredly.

"Why don't I have one of the drivers take you home to rest and we'll do dinner instead of lunch when I get home," Ebony suggested.

"Only if we go to Chayse's Place." Mama Ellis grinned.

"It's a date."

After Ebony had Dane call for one of the company drivers to meet them in front of the building, she helped Mama Ellis gather her bags. Just as they walked out of Ebony's office, Mama Ellis halted midstride.

"Ebony...something's wrong." Mama Ellis dropped the bag she was carrying and took a staggering step forward before collapsing to the floor.

❖

Belinda Jansen pressed play on her stereo remote, turned up the volume to the loudest level reasonable without disturbing her neighbors, let the soothing sounds of her meditation playlist surround her, and then took a sip of her chamomile tea. This was the first day of her long-awaited vacation week of self-imposed seclusion. After the past four months with an overly demanding client who had her reconsidering her career as a private nurse, all she wanted to do was retreat into her own little world of relaxation, reading, and junk food with no human contact whatsoever. Just as Belinda picked up the warm, gooey cinnamon bun she'd made for breakfast, her cell phone buzzed beside her. She eyed the glistening frosting slowly oozing its way down the bun and decided to let the call go to voice mail. A minute later, her phone buzzed again so she glanced down and saw the picture of her father's face on the screen and couldn't help but smile.

"Hey, Daddy," she answered.

"Hey, baby girl, sorry to bother you on your day off," he said.

"You know I don't mind when you call," she said.

"I hope you still feel that way after I ask a favor," he said hesitantly.

Belinda chuckled. "Hmm...is it that bad?"

"Well, depends on how you look at it," he answered cryptically.

"I'm almost afraid to ask. What's up?"

"I have a very special patient who's heading home in a few days after suffering a stroke. She's going to need home care for a few months, and her family wants the best, no matter the cost, and asked if I would recommend someone. Of course I recommended you."

"Daddy..." Belinda said tiredly.

"I know you're on vacation," he hurried to finish before she could say more, "but this patient really is someone special, and I can't see trusting her and her family in the hands of anyone else besides my daughter."

Belinda's father rarely asked for favors, especially when it came to both of their jobs, so the fact that he was calling when he knew she rarely took time off, and asking this was a big thing. She gazed longingly at her now cooled honey bun and sighed in resignation.

"Okay, but only because this is so important to you," she said.

"Thanks, baby girl, I knew I could count on you. I owe you big time," he said.

"Sunday dinner at Chayse's?"

Her father chuckled. "You got it."

He gave her the name and number of who to call before telling her how much he loved her and good-bye. Belinda looked at the paper she'd written everything on and shook her head. She adored her father and found she couldn't say no to him because he so rarely asked her for anything. She didn't think she'd ever be able to show him how much she appreciated everything he'd done for her after they'd lost her mother to breast cancer when Belinda was just eight years old. By the time her mother had been diagnosed it was already at Stage 4 and the only thing they could do was make those last few years she had with them ones to remember. They had been a mutual support system to each other through their grief.

Before she could change her mind, she picked up her phone and dialed the number.

"Pure Music Studios, how may I help you?" a pleasant male voice answered.

"Hello, may I speak with Ms. Trent?" Belinda asked.

"May I ask who is calling?"

"My name is Belinda Jansen. Dr. Richard Jansen referred me."

"Oh yes, you're the private nurse. I'm Dane, Ms. Trent's assistant. She's been expecting your call. Are you available to meet this afternoon?"

"This afternoon?" Belinda asked. She was hoping to at least be able to enjoy one day of her vacation.

"Yes, it will have to be this afternoon. Ms. Trent will clear her calendar for whatever time works best for you."

"Will three work?" Belinda asked, hoping this wasn't another pushy and demanding client.

"Yes, that works fine," Dane gave her the address of the office and ended the call with an abrupt but pleasant good-bye.

Belinda laid her head against the back of the chair, closed her eyes, and took a few deep breaths to try to quell the beginnings of a tension headache when a thought occurred to her. When her father gave her the name of her prospective client, she hadn't given it a second thought, but now she connected it with the name of the company she'd called to reach her. Her client was The Beast, a hip-hop artist from back in the day who was now a producer.

Belinda recalled reading about her recently in some magazine about how she was a really private person, almost reclusive, refusing to give interviews and rarely attending industry events. She had even been in the news over the past few years for getting into a few scuffles with paparazzi.

Belinda sighed tiredly, that's all she needed, a job working with an egomaniacal celebrity.

❖

Ebony was gazing out the large bank of windows behind her desk, her mind was going over everything that was being completed for Mama Ellis's homecoming. Per the doctor's instructions, Ebony was having Mama Ellis's level of their brownstone renovated to accommodate her medical needs, one of which included installing an elevator so that she wouldn't have to use the stairs to come up to either her or Sheree's floors whenever she wanted to. The elevator wouldn't be finished for another month, but everything else would be completed by tomorrow. The only thing she had left to do was hire a nurse who she was waiting to interview. Just as she looked down at her watch for the time, Dane buzzed her on the intercom.

"E, your three o'clock has arrived. Should I bring her in?"

"Yeah, thanks, Dane."

A moment later, Dane walked in followed by a woman Ebony could only describe as stunning. She wore a navy blue business suit that was tailored perfectly for her curvaceous hourglass figure, an ivory camisole top with a draped collar, gold hoop earrings, and a gold heart-shaped locket. The hem of the fitted skirt stopped just at the top of her knees, showing off a pair of smooth, long, shapely legs. She had a rich dark chocolate complexion, wore her locs in an intricately entwined upswept bun that emphasized her wide deep brown doe eyes, and full lush mouth that had Ebony wondering if they were as kissably soft as they looked. She walked toward Ebony with a confident stride and a natural sway to her hips, and as conservative as her style was, it couldn't hide her sensuality.

She offered Ebony her hand. "Good afternoon, Ms. Trent. I'm Belinda Jansen."

Ebony grasped her hand, liking the firm handshake she was given in return. "Thank you for coming on such short notice, Ms. Jansen. Can I have my assistant get you something to drink?"

"No, I'm fine, thank you," Belinda answered pleasantly.

"Please, have a seat." Ebony walked back to sit behind her desk.

Once they were both seated, Belinda reached into her briefcase to hand Ebony several papers. "As you will see from my résumé I have worked for a very prominent private nursing company for several years as well as partnered with Dr. Jansen's practice for over a year now. There are various referrals from some of his patients for your review."

Ebony took the papers, set them aside without even a glance, and leaned casually back in her chair. "No offense, Ms. Jansen, but I couldn't care less about what's said about you on paper. The only reason you're here is because you were highly recommended by Dr. Jansen. I've trusted his opinion for several years now so I'm hoping this recommendation is not because you happen to be his daughter or that he gets a cut of whatever you make from his referrals. I'm assuming it's because you're good at what you do. If that's not the case, then we can save both of us a lot time by cutting this meeting short right now."

Belinda unflinchingly met Ebony's steely gaze with her own. "Ms. Trent, if you know my father then you know for a fact that he would not lightly recommend someone to assist one of his patients with their recovery unless he knew they would do a good job, whether it's his daughter or some other random nurse. Although I did come here as a favor to him, I am not so hard up for work that I will be devastated if you don't hire me," she said matter-of-factly. "Now, if you're looking for a professionally trained and experienced nurse who not only comes highly recommended from Dr. Richard Jansen but four other well-established doctors in the New York area and does this job because she loves it and not just for a paycheck, then you've found her. But if you're looking for someone to intimidate who'll be too impressed with who they're working for to do their job, well then, by all means, let's end this meeting and I'll enjoy the rest of what was supposed to be my week off."

Impressed and amused by Belinda's blunt and feisty manner, it took some serious restraint for Ebony not to smirk in response, but she managed to keep a straight face as she leaned forward to study this woman more closely.

"How does sixty dollars an hour, live-in Monday through Friday with weekends off work for you?" Ebony asked.

"That's acceptable," Belinda said.

Ebony stood. "Good. Be at the house tomorrow morning at nine a.m. so that you can get the layout of the place and get settled in before your patient comes home. Dane will give you all the details on your way out. Thank you again for coming, Ms. Jansen," she held her hand out across the desk toward Belinda.

Belinda stood and shook her hand. "I will see you tomorrow, Ms. Trent."

Upon Belinda's departure, Ebony sat back in her chair staring toward the door curiously. Nurse Jansen was definitely not what she expected. When she'd heard her last name, Ebony just assumed she was Dr. Jansen's sister or some other older relative. What she hadn't imagined was the young, curvaceous beauty who had walked into her office carrying herself with the confidence and pride of the Queen of Sheba. Ebony's attraction to her was instantaneous. All she could do as Belinda spoke with that smoky, seductive voice was imagine what she wore under her tailored suit and how long it would take to get her out of it. Only decades of keeping her emotions on the down-low kept her in check during the interview. It was a good thing Belinda would be staying with Mama Ellis because Ebony wasn't sure how she would've handled sleeping in the same apartment as the woman. She physically had to shake herself and try to get her thoughts refocused on business and away from the X-rated images running through her mind.

❖

In spite of her hesitancy about her new employer, Belinda arrived at Ebony's house promptly at eight fifty a.m. the next morning. She didn't want to give any reason for Ebony to regret hiring her. There were three intercom buttons, two labeled "TRENT" and a third labeled "ELLIS." She checked the information that Ebony's assistant had given her, but there was no mention of three tenants in the building. Taking a chance, she pressed the top button labeled "TRENT" and nervously waited for an answer.

"Hello. Can I help you?" a friendly female voice said over the intercom.

"Yes, I'm Belinda Jansen, Ms. Ebony Trent is expecting me."

"Oh, yes, I'll buzz you in and be right down," she said.

Seconds later, the door buzzed and Belinda walked into an alcove entryway that led to a small, tastefully decorated foyer with what looked like the original wood parquet flooring, an intricately carved staircase, and two beautiful sets of French doors on either side of the staircase. Her attention was brought to the sound of someone coming down the stairs, and she took a deep breath to calm her racing heart. In spite of what she told Ebony about not being easily intimidated, Ebony seemed to make her nervous. To Belinda's surprise, it wasn't Ebony who came skipping down the stairs, it was a young woman who Belinda assumed was the younger sister she'd read about in one of the few interviews Ebony had done some time ago. She seemed to be a petite, softer, younger version of her older sister.

"Hello, I'm Sheree Trent." She offered Belinda her hand in greeting.

Belinda shook her hand. "Hello, it's nice to meet you."

"I know you were expecting Ebony, but she had to take a call and asked me to show you around. I'll take you up to her apartment after the grand tour," Sheree explained.

"That's fine. Whatever works best for you and Ms. Trent," Belinda said.

"Ms. Trent…that so does not fit my sister." Sheree grinned in amusement, then led Belinda toward the French doors to the right of the staircase.

She took a small ring of keys from her pocket and unlocked the door that led to a nice size fitness room.

"Before Mama Ellis's stroke this room was pretty much Ebony's domain, but she reconfigured it so that we could fit the physical therapy equipment Dr. Jansen said you would need. Feel free to look around. If there's anything we're missing let us know and we'll get it for you," Sheree said.

"From what I can see you all were very thorough," Belinda said, impressed that they had obviously listened to her father's exact instructions. Many times, she would walk into a patient's home with nothing ordered because the patient's family assumed Belinda would do it for them, not realizing that their home needed to be reconfigured to accommodate things like a physical therapy table, walking rails, or exercise bike.

"That's good because there's nothing we wouldn't do for Mama Ellis," Sheree said affectionately.

"Well, it's obvious you care about her very much, and I will do my best to make sure she has a healthy recovery," Belinda promised.

"We will definitely hold you to that," Sheree said. "Now, let me show you Mama Ellis's apartment."

Belinda followed her out of the fitness room and across the foyer to the second set of French doors.

"This is Mama Ellis's domain," Sheree said.

The apartment was done in an open floor plan with high ceilings and decoratively carved wooden archways similar to the pattern in the foyer staircase separating each of the main rooms from the other. They entered into the living room, and from there you could see the dining room, kitchen, and a music room that held a beautiful baby grand piano. The rooms were uncluttered and airy with simple comfortable furnishings and decor colors of cream, browns, and oranges. To Belinda's surprise, walking rails were placed throughout the entire apartment but done in such a way that it seemed to be part of the décor rather than for medical assistance. Sheree led her down a hallway located behind the kitchen that had four doors, two on the right, one on the left and the last at the end of the hall.

"This is going to be the private elevator for Mama Ellis to be able to get to Ebony's and my apartments." Sheree pointed toward a door on the left. "Ebony's on the second floor and I'm on the third."

She opened the other two doors on the right, the first of which was a small bathroom with a shower, sink, and toilet, and the second was a comfortable guest room.

"This will be your room while you're here during the week. I know it's a bit on the small side, but we tried to make it as comfortable as possible for you," Sheree said apologetically.

"It's fine," Belinda assured her.

Sheree then led her to the door at the end of the hall. "This is Mama Ellis's room."

It was spacious with a sitting area, private bath, and a large picture window that looked out onto a small enclosed garden and patio.

"Her bed used to be by the window, but we thought it would be best to have it right next to the bathroom so that she didn't have to go all the way across the room to get to it. We also rearranged the furniture so that she could use it to get around the room instead of the railings. She's already going to hate seeing those in the rest of the apartment so we didn't want to ruin the comfort of her bedroom by putting them in here," Sheree explained. "Unless you think she'll need them in here."

"No, this should be fine," Belinda said.

"Before the stroke, Mama Ellis was very independent and this has really set a blow to her ego, so Ebony and I are trying our best to make sure the changes we have to make won't set her back emotionally," Sheree explained.

"I understand. It will be helpful if you could tell me about what Miss Ellis's life was like before her stroke so I know what we're working toward in her recovery."

Sheree shook her head. "I take it Ebony hasn't told you anything."

"Our interview was somewhat brief," Belinda said.

"That's Ebony, brief and to the point. Please don't judge her by her rough exterior. Growing up, she sacrificed a lot after our mother abandoned us. If it weren't for her and Mama Ellis, I wouldn't be where I am today. Unfortunately, the things she had to do to get us all to this point have made her a bit hard and cynical. Her bark is worse than her bite most of the time," Sheree said.

"I'll have to take your word on that," Belinda said.

Sheree chuckled. "I see she's already charmed you. We have some time before Ebony's call is finished, why don't we have a seat in the living room and I'll tell you about Mama Ellis."

Sheree and Belinda talked for almost an hour about the matriarch of their unconventional family. Miss Ellis seemed to be a pretty special woman, and Belinda understood why her father was so determined to make sure she got the best care possible. Their conversation was interrupted by Sheree's cell phone buzzing on the coffee table.

"It's Ebony. She's finished her call. I'll take you up. Just remember, her bark—"

"Is worse than her bite," Belinda finished.

"Exactly," Sheree said.

They climbed the stairs to the second floor landing where another set of French doors stood open and walked into an apartment with the same layout as the first floor, but that's where the similarities ended. Where Miss Ellis's apartment was warm, comfortable, and obviously lived in, Ebony Trent's apartment was modern minimalist straight out of a magazine spread. It was beautifully decorated in shades of beige and black with the original hardwood floors. There was nothing out of place or lying around, the kitchen countertops were even clutter-free. It was showroom perfect, as if no one lived in it. They made their way through the living room to what was Ebony's home office, which, décor wise, was a smaller replica of her work office. Belinda couldn't seem to connect the serious, almost cold and anal person Ebony appeared to be to the one that her sister and Miss Ellis obviously adored.

As they entered, Ebony came from behind her desk and reached a hand toward Belinda. "Nice to see you again, Ms. Jansen," she greeted her without a hint of warmth behind her expression or words.

Ebony cut an imposing figure at five ten with a stern expression, close shaven hair with sharp, sculpted edges, and dressed in a tight black silk T-shirt that emphasized her muscular physique. The black, sharply creased slacks she wore were perfectly tailored for her equally muscular hips and behind. Like her work office, her home office was designed in sharp angles and edges of chrome, black, and silver that led Belinda to wonder if the rumors of her new employer being a cold hard-ass were more true than the loving figure Sheree had spoke of.

Belinda refused to let Ebony intimidate her the way she had the other day. She smiled brightly and grasped Ebony's hand in return. "It's nice to see you as well, Ms. Trent."

"Okay, you two, enough with the formal titles. Since we're going to be practically living together at least five days a week over the next several months, I think you could manage speaking on a first-name basis," Sheree said in amusement.

Belinda didn't fail to notice the way Sheree completely ignored the warning look Ebony directed at her. She definitely liked this feisty young woman.

"I'm fine with that if you are," Belinda said to Ebony, silently noting that their hands were still clasped. The warmth and firm grip of Ebony's hand was sending those little flutters she'd experienced at their first meeting through her belly.

"Uh…yeah…that's cool." Ebony slowly released Belinda's hand. "Can I get you anything?" she asked.

"A glass of water would be fine, thank you," Belinda answered.

"I'll get it," Sheree said, quickly leaving the room.

"So did Sheree show you around? Is there anything we need to get before Mama Ellis comes home?" Ebony asked as she walked back behind her desk.

"Yes, she did, and you're more than prepared for Miss Ellis's return home. Sheree has told me so much about her. I truly look forward to helping with her recovery."

Even though Ebony was touched by the sincerity in Belinda's voice she was more annoyed by the effect Belinda was having on her. "You're already hired, Ms. Jansen, so you don't need to impress me with compliments." She completely ignored the agreement to call each other by their first names

"Look, Ms. Trent, I don't know what I've done or said, but it's obvious you and I are not going to get along so maybe it's best if you find another nurse. I'd be glad to refer you to someone who's been doing this much longer than I have and who is very discreet due to her prominent clientele," Belinda said.

"Belinda, you are not going anywhere," Sheree walked into the room, handing her a glass of water. "And, Eb, stop being so rude. Mama Ellis would tear you a new one if she heard you speaking that way to a guest in this house.

"Belinda, I apologize for my sister. She tends to take her Beast persona a little too seriously," Sheree said then turned back to Ebony. "I need to go by the shelter. Can I trust you to tone it down for Mama Ellis's sake?" she asked Ebony.

"Yeah, go ahead. I'll be fine," she said.

"I'm serious, Eb. I like Belinda and I know Mama Ellis will also, so she better still be here when I get back."

"Don't push it, Sheree," Ebony warned her gently.

Sheree grinned knowingly, then walked over and gave Ebony a sisterly peck on the cheek. "Don't forget it's your turn to cook tonight. Bye, Belinda," she said as she walked out.

"Did you bring your personal belongings or do you need to go back home and get them?" Ebony asked.

"I brought my things with me since you wanted me to get settled in before Miss Ellis returned home," Belinda answered.

"Good." She opened one of her desk drawers and grabbed a ring of keys. "These are keys to the front and back entrances, to all of our apartments, and the fitness room. Sheree and I usually keep our doors unlocked so that Mama Ellis can come and go, but I'm giving you copies just in case." Ebony handed the keys to Belinda.

"I assume this means I'm still hired," Belinda said.

"You heard my sister," Ebony said in answer.

They spent some time discussing Belinda's contract, schedules, and Mama Ellis's treatments and recovery, but underneath the polite conversation Ebony felt her attraction growing for Belinda She managed to maintain her cool as Belinda's intoxicating vanilla scent almost drove her to distraction. She couldn't believe that as Belinda casually talked about the best therapy for recovering stroke patients she was wondering if Belinda's lips were as soft as they looked and how it would feel to let loose her entwined locs so she could run her fingers through them. Each time she realized where her thoughts were going she silently chastised herself for losing sight that this was about Mama Ellis, not her own usually controlled but suddenly rampant sex drive. Besides, Nurse Jansen was probably straight as an arrow.

Belinda was finding it difficult to keep her thoughts away from the woman before her, wondering how Ebony's firm calloused hands would feel stroking her, if her muscular body was as sexy without clothes as it was in them. Belinda blamed it on the fact that she hadn't had a date in six months or sex since she and her ex broke up almost a year ago.

Fortunately, she was given a reprieve when Ebony's cell phone interrupted their conversation. Ebony answered, spoke briefly, then brought her attention back to Belinda.

"I have to take this. Is there anything else we need to discuss before tomorrow?" Ebony asked.

"No, I think we've covered everything," Belinda said as she stood.

"Good. Like I mentioned earlier, we usually have dinner down at Mama Ellis's apartment so I'll be down around four to start cooking before Sheree gets home. You're welcome to join us, but I'm sure you've got a life outside of work so don't feel obligated to stay," Ebony said.

"I do have some errands to run, but I'll probably be back by then. Is there anything I can get you while I'm out?" Belinda asked.

"No, thank you, Ms. Jan—Belinda."

"You're welcome, Ebony," Belinda said with a smile as she walked out.

Belinda returned from her errands later than expected after stopping by her father's office to pick up a copy of Miss Ellis's medical history to look over tonight rather than having him bring it by the next day when she returned home. As she entered the foyer, the door to Miss Ellis's apartment was open and the soothing sound of piano jazz followed by the aromatic scent of grilled steak drifted toward her. She walked in to find Ebony in the kitchen dressed in jeans, a black V-neck T-shirt, and an apron with a large lipstick kiss imprint that said "Kiss the Cook or Else..." It was so charmingly unexpected that Belinda couldn't help but chuckle to herself.

Ebony looked up as she approached the kitchen. "Sheree just called. She's going to be out later than she expected and won't be home for dinner so I thought I'd finish it up and then just take mine up to my apartment so I won't bother you."

"Please don't feel obligated to leave on my account. I won't mind having the company," Belinda said.

Ebony stared at her for a moment then cleared her throat and grabbed a platter off the counter. "Uh…okay…Let me just go check the steaks on the grill." She hurried out a door in the kitchen that led to the enclosed yard.

Belinda realized that she had suggested dinner alone with Ebony. They barely made it through the two business-related meetings they had already without Ebony's unprovoked dislike for her causing tension; how were they going to make it through a casual dinner?

Ebony returned with steaks still sizzling on the platter. "I already set the table. I was just waiting for the steaks to finish."

"Okay. Let me just drop these bags off and I'll be right out," Belinda said.

She walked to the guest room, dropped her shopping bags and backpack onto the bed, then stopped in the bathroom to wash her hands. As she did, she found herself gazing into the mirror above the sink to check her hair and what little makeup she wore, then stopped herself.

"Stop it! It's dinner with your client, not a date," she reprimanded her reflection.

After taking a deep breath to settle the fluttering in her belly, she walked out of the bathroom. As she reached the dining room, Ebony was just setting a bottle of white wine on the table.

"I didn't know what you would like," she said apologetically. "There's also beer, soda, or iced tea, if you prefer, and I can throw a salmon steak on the grill if you don't eat meat."

"The wine will be good, and I never say no to a good steak," Belinda said as she sat at the place setting across from Ebony.

When Ebony actually smiled Belinda's heart skipped a beat as that small gesture softened Ebony's face so much she almost looked like a different person. It was gone just as quickly as it had come, as if Ebony hadn't realized she'd done it until too late. To Belinda's disappointment, it was replaced by a frown as Ebony sat and began filling her plate with food.

"You know, you should do that more often." Belinda reached for the wine bottle.

Ebony glanced at her in confusion. "Do what?"

"Smile. It's not going to make you any less tough than you already are."

Ebony's brow raised in question. "You've been here for one day and you think you know me already?"

"No, I can only go by what I've seen since we first met yesterday. This is really good," Belinda said as she tried a slice of the steak. "Do you use a marinade or dry rub?"

Ebony laid her silverware down gazing intently at Belinda. "It's a special marinade Mama Ellis uses, and what have you learned about me in this short time that makes you think you know me so well?"

Belinda set her silverware down. If she was going to get herself fired on the first day she might as well go out with guns blazing.

"Okay, just remember you asked," Belinda said. "You're a control freak with a hint of compulsive disorder. You believe that your 'Beast' persona is the only reason people take you seriously when you actually depend on it yourself to hide behind and mask your own insecurities. Unless they're in your immediate circle, you rarely let people in. If you do allow someone into the circle it's only on the surface because you know it's only a matter of time before they do something to prove that you can't trust them. Unfortunately, the only people who get to see the real you, the devoted, sensitive, caring you, are the other two people who share this house with you."

Belinda waited, nervously watching the tic that appeared in Ebony's right jaw and bracing herself for the storm that was about to blow. The last thing that she expected to happen was for a smirk to appear on Ebony's face followed by a burst of laughter. Belinda watched her in wide-eyed surprise.

"Well, that certainly wasn't the reaction I expected, not that I'm complaining," Belinda said.

"Well, let's call it even because that wasn't what I expected you to say. That hit a little too close to home," Ebony said.

"I apologize if I overstepped any boundaries." Belinda was hesitant to relax her guard. She found herself comparing Ebony to a landscape puzzle where there's so much detail that you can't tell one puzzle piece from the next unless you really pay attention to matching the shapes of the pieces within the puzzle. Belinda had always been good at puzzles, and she was beginning to piece together what made this complex woman tick. The extent Ebony had gone to to make sure Miss Ellis was well taken care of, the immense love that showed on her face when she spoke to her sister, the obvious time and care she took in preparing dinner, the unexpected laughter rather than anger in reaction to what Belinda said about her, combined with the serious, philosophical street thug persona of The Beast made up one intriguing and sexy puzzle.

"No need to apologize. Like you said, I asked." Ebony picked up her silverware and continued to eat.

After a moment, Belinda did the same. They ate in silence with Ebony glancing curiously at Belinda every now and then. Oddly enough, the fact that she called Ebony out on all of her issues quicker than the court mandated psychiatrist she had to go to for six months a few years ago after getting into several fights, attracted her even more to Belinda. She was the first woman in a long time who didn't either quake in her boots from fright or fawn all over her trying to get in her bed or wallet.

"You're a very good cook," Belinda said.

Ebony shrugged. "Sheree and I couldn't survive off of PB&J and Chunky soup forever so Mama Ellis taught me how to cook," she said as if having to raise her sister alone wasn't a big deal.

"I read the interview you did for *XXL* magazine a few years ago. I admire what you did. Not every sixteen-year-old could take on the responsibility of raising a young sibling while staying under the radar of children services," Belinda said.

"What's there to admire," Ebony said, a little embarrassed by the praise. "I did what I had to do, what my mother couldn't do." She suddenly stood feeling uncomfortable with where the discussion was leading. "Are you finished?" she asked

"Yes, but please, let me help. After all, you did the cooking," Belinda offered.

"All right," Ebony said.

They had the table cleared in just a few trips. As Ebony packed the leftovers into containers, she looked behind her and almost dropped the salad bowl as she was greeted with the sight of Belinda's firm, round behind as she bent over to load the dishwasher. As Ebony juggled the dish to keep it from falling to the floor, she jammed her finger on the counter and set the bowl down with a hiss of pain.

"Are you all right?" Belinda rushed over to her.

"I'm fine!" Ebony snapped through clenched teeth.

Belinda held her hand out to Ebony. "Let me see."

"I said I was fine."

Belinda gave Ebony a look that told her she was not the one to argue with. Without another word, Ebony laid her hand in Belinda's. As Belinda lowered her head to gently examine and prod her finger, the scent of her hair oil drifted up to Ebony who closed her eyes and breathed in the cocoa and shea butter scent as if it were the most wonderful smell ever. It took her a second to realize Belinda had asked her a question. Ebony quickly blinked her eyes open and found Belinda gazing at her in concern.

"Uh…what?"

"I asked if your finger hurts."

"No, not really. Just throbbing a little now," Ebony said.

"It's not broken, but you should probably put some ice on it just in case it swells," Belinda told her.

"I'll be fine," Ebony said, not realizing she had been drawing closer to Belinda until she found their lips just inches apart.

She was just about to pull back when Belinda closed the gap and pressed her lips against Ebony's. The kiss was tentative for just a moment, then slowly erupted into an aching, burning passion the longer it went on. When Belinda laid her hands on Ebony's chest Ebony grasped her hips and brought them flush against her own. Ebony had never felt anything like what she was feeling at that moment as she allowed her own desire to take over where common sense had once ruled. She didn't care that she had no idea who Belinda truly was or that she was in her employ. The inner beast that she'd managed to tame was rearing its horny head, and she had no desire to stop it.

Belinda was not only surprised by what was happening but also by the fact that she didn't want it to stop. Her body was responding to Ebony in a way it had not responded to any of her previous lovers. Not even her ex-girlfriend Carla's extensive talents as a lover could make Belinda respond so passionately to just a kiss. Belinda wrapped her arms around Ebony's neck as Ebony backed her up against the counter to bring their whole bodies flush against one another.

Ebony slid her lips from Belinda's, kissing her way along her jawline, and nipped her earlobe, growling sexily in her ear. "Tell me to stop."

Belinda's head was saying stop this nonsense immediately, but the sensations rolling through her body as Ebony's firm lips traveled along her neckline into her cleavage refused to listen and left her without the ability to speak. Ebony took her silence as permission to continue and ran the tip of her tongue along the rounded low cut edge of her shirt's cleavage as she simultaneously slid her hands up under the hem of the shirt to stroke Belinda's already hardened nipples through her bra. Within a matter of seconds, Belinda's shirt was unbuttoned and lay open to give Ebony better access to her breasts.

"Mmm...you are so sexy," Ebony said.

She didn't give Belinda a moment to think before she rained passion down once again through her lips. After one more passionate kiss, Ebony cupped Belinda's behind, lifted her up, wrapped her legs around her waist, and carried her to the guest bedroom without breaking her stride. She laid her on the bed, sweeping the bags Belinda had laid there earlier onto the floor as she did. Ebony paused, waiting with bated breath. This was when most women changed their mind. When they realized that Ebony was far more than they bargained for. When her true beast, her beast of desire, came forward, they ran in the other direction. For just a second, she saw that fear in Belinda's eyes before it was quickly shoved aside by the same desire that matched her own.

As Ebony loomed over her, Belinda could see why she was called The Beast. The raw hunger Belinda saw in Ebony's eyes made her feel as if she would eat her alive and suck the bones dry before she was satisfied.

Belinda grasped Ebony's head, bringing it slowly down toward hers. "Tell me to stop."

A low growl rumbled up from Ebony's chest as she lowered her head the rest of the way to give Belinda the kiss she wanted. Belinda didn't hold back, practically devouring Ebony with burning lips, dueling tongue, and gentle nips. Belinda couldn't get her clothes off fast enough. Ebony tried to help, but it seemed as if as soon as Belinda bared the slightest bit of flesh Ebony was tasting and touching, driving Belinda to distraction.

Finally, when the last of Belinda's clothing was discarded, Ebony stepped away from the bed and said, "Take your hair down. All I've been thinking about since you walked into my office was to see you lying naked before me with your hair spread out on the pillow."

Belinda knelt on the bed as she removed the pins holding her hair and untangled the locs so that they flowed almost to her waist and around her like a veil. She then lay down and spread them out on the pillow just as Ebony asked.

"Damn, girl," Ebony said in awe.

"Do I get what I've been fantasizing about since I met you?" Belinda asked.

"And what would that be?" Ebony asked as she walked toward the bed.

Belinda rolled onto her side and propped her head on her hand. "To see if you look as good naked as you do clothed."

Ebony smiled as she backed away from the bed again and began to undress. Belinda thoroughly enjoyed every bit of the slow striptease show Ebony was giving her. Ebony's body was broad but sculpted and there didn't seem to be an ounce of fat on her muscular frame. With her close-shaven hair, fit body, and intense expression, she made one hell of a sexy stud. Belinda's palms itched in anticipation of touching Ebony's body. As Ebony tossed her boxer briefs to the side, she slowly walked toward the bed, her sleek muscular body moving like that of a panther stalking its prey.

As she climbed onto the bed and crouched over Belinda on all fours she asked, "Do you like what you see?"

Belinda reached down, grabbed one of Ebony's hands, and placed it at the juncture of her thighs. "You tell me."

Ebony slid her hand down the smoothly waxed mound to the entrance of Belinda's vagina, holding eye contact while she slipped a long index finger inside. Belinda's eyes fluttered closed as she moaned deeply with pleasure.

"Open your eyes," Ebony commanded. "I want you to watch everything I do to you."

As Belinda watched, Ebony brought her finger up to her lips, her long, thick tongue circling her finger, and licked every bit of Belinda's juices off it. Belinda almost climaxed right then.

With a mischievous grin Ebony said, "Not yet. You'll come when I want you to."

Belinda's common sense spoke up once again, telling her to run. That this was not like her. She didn't have sex with strangers. It took four months for Carla to get in her pants and here she was dripping wet and moaning in bed with a woman she just met yesterday.

Ebony saw the hesitancy in Belinda's expression and hoped it was short-lived. After what she'd seen in Belinda's eyes earlier, she didn't want to turn back now. Something about that moment had her believing they had a common hunger that could not be easily appeased.

She leaned forward, placed her lips along Belinda's ear, and whispered, "I have nothing to serve you but pleasure. Let me feed your passion. Let me ease that hunger I know you're feeling because I'm feeling it too."

Belinda moaned in response. Ebony felt the tension leave Belinda's body, felt Belinda's nipples harden and brush along her forearm as she writhed beneath her, and she knew she'd won the battle. She looked down and Belinda's half-lidded gaze met hers.

"Remember, eyes open," Ebony commanded.

Ebony grasped Belinda's hands and placed them above her head as she nipped, kissed, and touched her way down Belinda's body from her lips, to her neck, pausing to pay homage to both of her breasts, down her midriff, until she reached the juncture of her thighs. There Ebony gently spread Belinda's legs, settled down between them, and looked up to make sure she was watching to find Belinda's eyes heavy-lidded with desire. Ebony lowered her head just enough to do what she wanted to do while also focusing on Belinda's eyes.

Ebony smoothed her hands down Belinda's sides, grasping her hips as the tip of her tongue slowly teased along and dipped into Belinda's slick opening. Ebony's tongue dove in and out of Belinda as her inner walls began contracting, rewarding Ebony with more of the sweet nectar she was craving. Belinda moaned, throwing her head back as her body began to quake with the start of her orgasm. Ebony suddenly stopped and Belinda writhed and groaned in frustration and then looked down the length of her body at Ebony.

With a mischievous grin, Ebony said, "You looked away so I assumed you wanted to stop."

Belinda propped herself up on her forearms and focused her gaze on Ebony who, satisfied with Belinda's action, then lay back down and continued her ministrations. It didn't take long for Ebony to have Belinda riding that orgasmic wave once again with her tongue continuing to manipulate Belinda's pussy as her fingers traveled down to join in the fun by massaging her hardened clit. Ebony could see stubborn determination keeping Belinda's gaze locked onto Ebony's as she felt Belinda's body tense as an orgasm slammed into her body not once but twice. Ebony moaned into Belinda's pussy as her own body responded to the raw ecstasy in Belinda's eyes with an orgasm that ripped through her and ended in a pool of wetness between her own legs.

Belinda's strength finally fled, and she collapsed back onto the bed as little tremors rocked her body from the aftershock of the intense pleasure Ebony gave, and continued to give, as she leisurely licked Belinda clean. Once Ebony had her fill, she slid her hard body up along Belinda's until her face hovered just above hers and lowered her lips for a gentle kiss. Once the kiss ended, Belinda slowly opened her eyes and was met with such a look of tenderness from Ebony it caught her breath, but it was quickly replaced with the dark intensity she seemed to already have gotten used to and was no longer intimated by. Ebony moved to lie beside Belinda, who maneuvered her position so that she lay with her back spooned against the front of Ebony.

It was obvious Ebony didn't want to talk about what just happened, and since Belinda wasn't sure herself of what to say about how they ended up in bed together so quickly, she didn't fight it and allowed herself to relax within Ebony's strong embrace. She closed her eyes and, after the long day she had, it wasn't long before she drifted off to sleep.

Ebony lay there, her face buried within the cocoon of Belinda's locs as she slept, amused by the light snores mingled with the steady rise and fall of Belinda's breathing. So many thoughts were running through her mind that she knew she wouldn't sleep at all. She lay holding Belinda's soft curves against her body for a few more minutes then gently slid out of the bed, walked over to the closet, took a blanket down from the top shelf, took one last look at Belinda's beautiful body, then covered her before grabbing her clothes and walking out of the bedroom. Once she was dressed she finished cleaning the kitchen as quietly as possible then made sure everything was turned off and locked up as she left the apartment. Thinking Sheree hadn't returned home yet, she left the foyer and porch light on and trudged up the stairs to her own apartment. Ebony was startled when she found Sheree sitting at her kitchen counter with a glass of wine.

"Damn, Sheree, you trying to give me a heart attack?" Ebony said in irritation.

"No, but if I did it would be well-deserved," Sheree said angrily.

Ebony walked over to her fridge and grabbed a bottle of water. "Look, whatever is bothering you can we talk about it in the morning? I'm too tired for this right now."

Sheree ignored her. "You couldn't even keep it in your pants just this one time? Not even for Mama Ellis?"

Ebony closed the refrigerator door and leaned heavily against it. "How'd you know?"

"I came home and saw Mama Ellis's door open and heard voices. I figured you guys were still having dinner, but when I walked in I realized the voices were coming from the guest room and it was obviously not something I wanted to interrupt," she said.

"Why would you do something like that? I thought you were past all of that bullshit, the fights and the promiscuous sex. I would've at least thought you learned your lesson after the last time you did something like this with the interior designer for your apartment. It almost got you sued for sexual harassment. You could've at least given her time to get Mama Ellis on the road to recovery before you screwed it up by seducing her."

Ebony stood quietly, her head lowered. Confronted with Sheree's angry and confused expression she couldn't find the words to explain what happened. She had no idea how things got out of hand so quickly with Belinda. She simply shrugged and lowered her head again, too ashamed to meet Sheree's eyes.

Sheree grabbed her wine glass and the expensive bottle of wine she'd taken from Ebony's stash, and stood to leave. "You better fix this by the time we bring Mama Ellis home tomorrow afternoon, Eb. I've spoken to some of Belinda's past clients and they have nothing but high praise for her. I think Belinda is one of the best home care nurses available so you need to figure out how to make this work, for Mama Ellis's sake," she said before walking out of the apartment.

The next morning, Belinda woke early relieved to find herself alone in bed. She wasn't sure how she was going to face Ebony after what happened last night, and she needed time to gather her thoughts before she did. She did know one thing, if she was going to continue to work for this family what happened last night could absolutely not happen again, no matter how mind-blowing it was, and there was no question about that, it was definitely mind-blowing. Belinda blushed at the memory of how uninhibited she had been. Her past lovers wouldn't recognize the passionate, multi-orgasmic woman she had been with Ebony. Hell, she barely recognized herself while it was happening. Just thinking about Ebony's hands and tongue on and in her brought an aching throb between her legs that almost had her moaning with need. Belinda squeezed her thighs together until the feeling passed, and with a shuddering sigh of relief, forced herself to get out of bed to prepare herself for the repercussions of last night.

After a quick shower, she put on one of her nursing uniforms, a pair of hot pink scrub pants and a black leopard scrub top with hot pink embroidered trim. She didn't think wearing street clothes was appropriate but also hated the sterile look of a traditional nurse's uniform and scrubs so when she discovered Heartsoul's nontraditional and colorful scrubs, she was hooked. She believed it helped ease her patients' discomfort when she looked less like a strict, serious nurse. Once Belinda was dressed, she twisted and wound her locs into a secure bun at the nape of her neck, trying not to think of the hunger in Ebony's eyes when she'd lain down and spread her locs out the way Ebony had requested. Finally, after taking a deep, cleansing breath, she left the bedroom to tackle cleaning the kitchen since they never managed to finish it last night.

To her surprise, it was spotless, as if some magical fairy had erased any sign of their dinner. Belinda didn't need to wonder who that fairy had been because she couldn't imagine as compulsive as Ebony was that she would leave the kitchen a mess. Her thoughts were interrupted by a knock on the apartment door. She knew it could only be one of two people, and her heart beat frantically in her chest at the thought of it being Ebony. She walked to the door and could tell through the sheer curtains that it was Sheree. She tried not to look disappointed as she opened the door.

"Good morning! I've come bearing gifts," Sheree said as she held up a bag with the wonderful aroma of baked goods and a cup holder with two coffee cups.

Sheree's warm personality was contagious, and Belinda couldn't help but smile as well. "Good morning. C'mon in." She stepped aside to let Sheree in.

Sheree headed toward the kitchen counter. "I remembered from our conversation yesterday that you like green tea instead of coffee in the morning so I picked some up along with some muffins and bagels fresh from the bakery oven."

"Thank you. You didn't have to go to all that trouble," Belinda said as she grabbed a couple of plates from the cabinet.

"It was no trouble at all. I usually stop and pick up coffee and bagels a couple of times a week on my way back from my morning run," Sheree explained.

"Is there anything you need for Mama Ellis's return?" she asked.

"No, I think I'm covered. You and Ebony have been very thorough in getting the equipment I need. Dr. Jansen gave me her records yesterday and, based on the dietician's recommendations, I've set up a weekly delivery of her meals for the first month so that we can focus on her physical recovery," Belinda explained.

"Okay. Ebony will also have her cleaning service coming in twice a week so you won't have to worry about that. I'm sure you could tell by her apartment that they're very thorough," Sheree said.

"She is definitely neat."

"Neat is an understatement."

They were both laughing when Ebony walked in. "Am I interrupting?"

"No, we're just having a little breakfast. I brought you a bran muffin," Sheree said.

Ebony strolled over to the counter and sat on one of the stools beside her sister. "G'morning," she greeted Belinda cautiously.

"Good morning. I noticed orange juice in the fridge yesterday. Would you like a glass?" she asked.

Ebony's brow furrowed worriedly. "Uh, yeah, thanks."

Sheree and Ebony watched Belinda casually take a glass from the cabinet, fill it with orange juice, and slide it across the counter to Ebony.

"What time should I expect you all back with Miss Ellis?" Belinda asked Sheree as she casually sipped her tea.

"We should be home by three p.m. I went to visit her yesterday while I was out and told her all about you, which, from what she told me, there was no need to. I guess having your father for her doctor gave her the advantage of having the down-low on you before we did."

Belinda blushed. "My father is very talkative."

"And very proud of his daughter. You already have Mama Ellis's approval without even having met her so I guess you're here to stay, isn't that right Ebony?" Sheree said.

Ebony frowned at Sheree. "What made you think she wouldn't stay?"

"You two didn't seem to get along very well when Belinda first arrived so I was worried your curmudgeon ways would scare her off," Sheree said.

Ebony's and Belinda's gaze met across the counter.

"I think we all want the same thing and that's to help Miss Ellis make a full recovery. Whatever…feelings…or dislikes we have for each other will have to be put aside in order for that to happen," Belinda said, hoping Ebony understood and agreed with her.

Ebony's gaze narrowed angrily as it held Belinda's. Belinda forced herself not to turn away. She had to make Ebony believe that last night meant nothing but a casual fling to her, in spite of the fact that her body's reaction the moment Ebony walked into the apartment said otherwise.

After a tense moment, Ebony pushed her untouched muffin and orange juice away and stood. "I've got some things to take care of before we go to the hospital. I'll see you later," she said then turned and left the apartment.

❖

Ebony looked at her computer screen where she had Belinda's Facebook, Twitter, and Instagram pages open feeling like a stalker. Since she wasn't a "Friend" or "Follower" she wasn't able to obtain much information. She learned that Belinda was single, well educated, had less than one hundred friends, three of which she and Ebony had in common—Sheree, one of Ebony's former lovers, and one of Ebony's closest friends, Chayse Carmichael. She picked up her phone, texted Sheree that she'd meet her at the hospital, grabbed a baseball cap and sunglasses, and then left the apartment. Ebony arrived at her destination twenty minutes later, Chayse's Place, a soul food restaurant in Harlem.

Ebony was greeted by the tall, leggy, redhead who manned the hostess stand. "Hey, Ebony! It's been a while," she said.

"Hey, Raquel, is Chayse in yet?" she asked.

"Yes, she's in the kitchen." Raquel waved over one of the waiters.

"Please go in the kitchen and let Chayse know she has a visitor," she told him then turned her attention back to Ebony. "I'm still waiting for that call."

"I've got a lot going on right now so I'm not really socializing at the moment," Ebony said, not really in the mood for Raquel's not-so-subtle flirting.

"You do look a little stressed. You know, I'm a licensed massage therapist. Why don't I come by later after my shift and help you relax." Raquel ran her fingers up Ebony's arm.

"Raquel, now you know Ebony isn't into vanilla no matter how tempting it is."

Ebony felt a sense of relief at Chayse's arrival. She'd turned down Raquel too many times to count, but the woman was determined to get into Ebony's bed.

"Can't blame a girl for trying," she said.

Chayse chuckled. "You gotta give her an A for persistence," she said, then turned and gave Ebony a grip and hug. "What's up, man, how's Mama Ellis doing?"

"She's doing much better. She's coming home today and is already asking when we can come here for Sunday brunch," Ebony said.

"You know she's always got a table waiting for her. When you get a chance email me her dietary needs while she's recovering and I'll whip up something and bring it by this weekend."

"I appreciate that, man. She'll love that," Ebony said.

"So, what's up? The workaholic you are, you obviously didn't stop by in the middle of the afternoon just to catch up," Chayse said knowingly.

Ebony looked down in embarrassment. "You got a few minutes?" she asked.

"Yeah, always for you. Why don't we sit out on the patio," Chayse suggested.

Ebony followed her through the restaurant to open sliding glass doors that led out to a small outdoor seating area. Once they were settled Ebony jumped right into what she had to say before she changed her mind.

"So we hired this home care nurse for Mama Ellis, and Sheree noticed you two were friends on Facebook so I just wanted to get some info about her, you know, to make sure we made the right decision in hiring her," Ebony said, instantly feeling guilty for adding Sheree's name to the lie.

"Who is she?" Chayse asked.

"Belinda Jansen."

"Belinda Jansen? Yeah, I know Belinda. We go way back."

"Really?" Ebony had to fight off the sudden rush of jealousy at the look on Chayse's face when she mentioned Belinda's name.

"No, man, it's not like that. We went to high school together, and I won't lie, I did have one of those school girl crushes for her, but she wasn't out at that time. After high school I didn't see her again until three years ago when she started volunteering with the same AIDS support group I provide weekly meals for. We've been good friends ever since," Chayse explained.

"You never tried to push up on her all this time?" Ebony asked.

"No. Unlike you, I don't need to seduce every sista that smiles at me," Chayse said jokingly. "All kidding aside, you couldn't have chosen a better caretaker for Mama Ellis. Not only is Belinda great at what she does, but she's also a wonderful, caring person. You already know what a great doctor her father is, and I'm sure he's the one who recommended her so what could I possibly tell you that he, or any of her previous clients, haven't told you already?"

"She's going to be living in my house five days a week. I just want to make sure she isn't going to rob me blind while we're at work or something," Ebony said.

Chayse had a way of looking at people as if she could see all the things you weren't telling her and she was giving Ebony that look right now.

"What's going on, Ebony? You and I both know you and Sheree have probably already gone through Belinda's references with a fine-tooth comb, especially after the interior designer incident, so why are you really asking about her?"

Ebony looked down, picking nervously at the edge of the tablecloth. She and Chayse had been friends since early in Ebony's career when her producer introduced them at a party. Ebony had been the one to loan Chayse the money to start her restaurant. She was the closest thing to a best friend Ebony ever had and probably knew more about her than anybody, including Sheree and Mama Ellis, but for some reason she was embarrassed to admit she might be falling for a woman she'd only met a few days ago. Ebony "The Beast" Trent had a reputation of being a womanizer; she didn't develop feelings. She barely spent more than a few weeks with one woman making sure they knew from day one that all she was looking for was a good time, nothing more, so they didn't get attached. For Belinda to have such a strong physical and emotional effect on her so quickly was scary, and Ebony never admitted being scared of anything. She wasn't going to start now.

"I was just curious." She slid her chair back to stand. "Thanks for the info. I'll send you Mama Ellis's dietary instructions when we get home from the hospital."

They walked back through the restaurant in companionable silence until they reached the entrance.

"You know you can call me if you need to talk," Chayse said.

"I know," Ebony said before walking out.

❖

Belinda finished arranging the flowers, balloons, and "Welcome Home" sign Sheree had dropped off before she left for the hospital and began preparing a light meal for everyone. Cooking was relaxing for her, and she'd been a bundle of nerves after the look Ebony gave her before she left this morning. It was the same look of hungry desire she'd given her last night, and it took all Belinda had not to melt into a puddle of mush in front of Sheree. An hour later, she was feeling more in control of herself after making broiled salmon, grilled garlic and herb chicken, a spinach salad, a fresh fruit platter, and a pitcher of water with lemon and lime slices, all prepared with Miss Ellis's diet restrictions in mind. Just as she laid everything out buffet style on the kitchen island, she heard voices outside. She walked out and opened the door just in time to hear Mama Ellis fussing at Ebony who was attempting to pick her up.

"I'm not an old cripple yet. It may take me a while, but I can walk up the stairs by my own self!" She swatted Ebony away from her and grabbed the railing with one hand and her cane with the other to maneuver up the first stair.

Ebony looked on worriedly, then noticed Belinda watching them from the top of the stairs. "What? You just gonna watch her fall and not do anything?"

Belinda knew Ebony wasn't intentionally trying to be nasty, but it still annoyed her just the same. She walked down the stairs to stand beside Mama Ellis who'd stopped on the second stair to catch her breath.

"Hello, Miss Ellis, I'm Belinda. Do you feel strong enough to manage the stairs alone or would you prefer someone helping you?"

"Child, I've been laid up in a bed for weeks, I'm barely strong enough to lift a finger, but I'm not gonna let that keep me from doing what I need to do."

Belinda smiled, liking her patient already. "Well, how about we compromise then. Why don't you take my hand and we'll do one step at a time at a slow and steady pace. That way you'll have accomplished your goal by not being carried up, and Ebony won't have to fire me."

Mama Ellis grinned then looked back at Ebony scowling up at them and Sheree smirking. "I like her," she said, then turned back to Belinda, handed her the cane she was using, then took her hand. "Let's do this. You two might as well go in. This is gonna take a while."

"I made something to eat for everyone if you'd like to wait for us in Miss Ellis's apartment," Belinda said over her shoulder then turned her focus to helping Mama Ellis.

Ebony opened her mouth to say something but was halted by Sheree. "Not everything has to be a fight, Eb. Mama Ellis told us to go in and wait so why don't we just do that."

Ebony turned her scowl on her sister who shrugged, grabbed Mama Ellis's bag, and left her standing in the middle of the sidewalk. She watched Belinda and Mama Ellis halt halfway up the stairs, then stalked angrily past them into the house. She paced back and forth in the middle of the living room, glancing toward the door every minute of the five it took Belinda and Mama Ellis to walk into the foyer. Seeing the tired and relieved smile on Mama Ellis's face, it took true restraint for Ebony not to run up to them and snatch Mama Ellis in her arms and carry her into her bedroom to rest.

"Are you all right?" she asked.

Mama Ellis waved her hand dismissively. "I'm fine, Eb. Now, stop worrying so much or you'll be the one in the hospital soon. Something sure smells good."

"It's this salmon Belinda made, Mama Ellis. It's bangin'!" Sheree said, sitting at the counter with a half-finished plate of food in front of her.

"Why don't you sit down, Miss Ellis, and I'll make you a plate." Belinda led her to the chair beside Sheree.

"Thank you, honey, and call me Mama Ellis." She patted Belinda's hand affectionately.

Ebony stared at the three of them as if they'd lost their minds as they chatted and laughed like it was just a normal day in the neighborhood. She didn't know what was pissing her off more, the fact that they were completely ignoring her or that they weren't taking any of the situation seriously.

"So you all are just gonna sit there like nothing is wrong? Like Mama Ellis didn't almost die? Am I the only one who hasn't lost their damn mind!" she said angrily.

"Well, since I didn't die and there's nothing wrong with me that Dr. Jansen and this talented nurse you hired can't help me recover from, then yes, we are just going to sit here enjoying each other's company and this delicious meal that was prepared for us, because judging from the welcome home sign, balloons, and flowers, this is supposed to be a party. Now you can grab a plate and join us or you can go upstairs and wallow in whatever funky mood you seem to be in." Mama Ellis scooped a spoonful of strawberries onto her plate.

Belinda caught Ebony's attention. "Ebony, may I speak with you in private." Without waiting for Ebony's reply, she walked toward the door leading out to the back patio.

Ebony walked out to find Belinda standing with her hands on her hips looking very annoyed.

"You need to school that temper of yours," she said.

"Who do you think you're talking to?" Ebony asked angrily.

"I'm obviously talking to you. I know you care about Mama Ellis and you're worried, but if you can't watch your temper then I'm going to ask that you not come around her for at least a week. I need her focused and in a positive state of mind when I start her physical therapy, and you throwing a tantrum when we don't act the way you expect us to will not help."

The look Ebony gave Belinda normally sent people scurrying from her path, but Belinda didn't flinch, she held her ground, meeting Ebony's hard stare with her own.

"Is that it?" Ebony asked.

"For now. She's probably starting to feel the effects of the day, especially after climbing the stairs, so I'm going to get her to lie down for an hour or so," Belinda said, walking past Ebony back into the house.

Ebony closed her eyes and took a deep breath, exhaling slowly, trying to get her mind and her heart to stop racing. She knew Belinda was right about her temper, but it scared her to think of losing Mama Ellis, and when Ebony was scared she lashed out. Sheree and Mama Ellis knew that about her, but it didn't make it right to make them the target for her outbursts.

She knew what she needed to do, but she never felt the need to really follow through with it, but seeing herself through Belinda's eyes was making her realize how it affected those close to her.

The sound of laughter from the kitchen brought her out of her reverie, but only the sound of Belinda's husky laugh made her heart skip a beat. Ebony realized she had unwittingly let Belinda in where no one but Sheree and Mama Ellis were. She found that she didn't just want to change for them but also for Belinda. She didn't want Belinda to see her as the cold and quick-tempered person everyone outside of her little circle saw her as because somehow, in these few short days, Belinda had managed to chip away a large piece of the wall Ebony had built around her heart the day she realized her mother had abandoned them, and she was slowly healing the wound left behind.

Ebony turned and walked back into the house, disappointed to find Belinda no longer there.

"She's getting Mama Ellis to rest," Sheree said.

Ebony walked over to the counter to pour a glass of the lemon water Belinda made. "I hadn't asked anything."

"You didn't have to. The look on your face when you walked in and she wasn't here said it all."

"What's that Cheshire cat grin for?" Ebony asked with a frown.

"This is more than just some superficial thing, isn't it?" Sheree asked.

Ebony didn't answer right away, gazing down into her glass of water as if the answer would suddenly float to the top.

"I honestly don't know," she answered then sat the glass down and walked out of the apartment.

❖

Belinda's alarm clock blared loudly on her nightstand. Moaning in frustration, she reached over to turn it off. She had already hit the snooze button twice which meant she was going to have to grab breakfast on her way uptown. She slowly made her way to the bathroom, still a bit groggy from a restless night of sleep filled with dreams of her and Ebony. It wouldn't have been so bad if it had been just this one dream, but it was just the latest of many that began shortly after the night they had sex. That had been three weeks ago.

Belinda figured the dreams would stop since there was never a repeat of that night. As a matter of fact, she barely saw Ebony since Mama Ellis had come home from the hospital, and when she did they were never alone. Ebony must have taken what she said about her temper to heart because she seemed much more easygoing. Oddly enough, the less she saw of Ebony the more frequent her dreams were, particularly during her weekends off spent in her own home. The dreams this time were different from the usual erotic dreams that woke her up wet, wanting, and blushing for days with just thoughts of what happened. This one left an ache in her heart rather than in between her legs.

Belinda was at a formal event dressed in a gold strapless dress and gold strappy high-heeled shoes with her locs wound into a chignon and entwined with sparkling gold-stringed crystals. She remembered feeling as if she was waiting for something but didn't know what until she saw Ebony walking toward her from across the room dressed in a black fitted tuxedo with a silk black shirt unbuttoned at the collar and smooth, shining black dress shoes. She smiled as she noticed the gold socks Ebony wore that matched her dress perfectly.

Ebony held out a hand toward Belinda as she drew near. "Dance with me," she'd said, and when Belinda placed her hand in Ebony's they were suddenly the only ones in the room. When Belinda stepped into Ebony's embrace she felt as if this was who she was made for. That everything she'd ever experienced had led her to this moment. It was then that she heard what song the DJ was playing. It was her parents' favorite song, "Sweet Love" by Anita Baker. It was shortly after that the sound of her alarm drowned out the lyrics and sent her dream fading into black. Even now, the memory of the dream was as vivid as it was while she slept, causing her heart to ache even more for the chance to go back to sleep and see the intensity of love in Ebony's eyes and the passion she'd felt being in Ebony's arms.

Just as Belinda stepped out of the shower, she heard the distant sound of her cell phone ringing. For anyone to be calling this early in the morning usually meant it was an emergency. She grabbed a towel and tried to hurry as carefully as possible so that she wouldn't slip on the tile and wood floors of her bathroom and apartment.

"Hello!" she said breathlessly into the phone.

"Uh, Belinda, it's Ebony."

Belinda's heart raced frantically in her chest. "Ebony? Is everything all right?"

"You sound a little winded. Did I call at a bad time?" Ebony asked.

"No, I was in the shower and had to run to get the phone."

"Oh. Well, everything is fine. I just wanted to let you know that I have to go out of town and won't be back until the weekend. I'm on my way to the airport now so I won't be at the house when you get there. Sheree has access to everything if you need anything for Mama Ellis."

"Okay. Thanks for calling to let me know."

"No problem. I'll see you next week," Ebony said, then hung up before Belinda could respond.

Belinda tossed her cell phone on the bed dejectedly. "What did you expect?" she asked herself out loud. "That she was calling to claim her undying love for you?"

She turned and retraced her wet footprints back into the bathroom to finish getting ready. An hour later, she was on the train heading uptown and trying to think of the best way to deal with her growing attraction to Ebony. They were too different, like oil and water. There would be no way they would mix. Yes, the sex was freaking awesome, but you couldn't build a lasting relationship on sex, and that's what Belinda wanted in her life now, a lasting relationship.

Ebony's womanizing reputation was well known, not only in the news but also within New York's gay community. Ebony was definitely not the committed relationship type. There was no shame in her game, and Belinda didn't want to be another conquest. Although, since she'd already slept with her it was probably a little too late to worry about that, but it wouldn't change the fact that she and Ebony were not meant to be.

When Belinda arrived at the Trent residence she felt she had made the right decision in not pursuing Ebony after that one night. Belinda also felt that Ebony being away would give her the space and time she needed to get thoughts of the sexy stud out of her head. Mama Ellis's apartment door was already open so Belinda walked in.

"Mama Ellis?" she called out.

"I'm in the garden," Mama Ellis cheerfully called back.

Belinda dropped her bag off in the guest room then went out to the garden through Mama Ellis's room.

"How are you feeling today?" she asked Mama Ellis as she sipped a cup of tea.

"I'm feeling good, honey. How was your weekend?" Mama Ellis asked.

"It was good. Had dinner with Daddy and Karen on Saturday, then met some friends for brunch on Sunday," she answered as she sat in the chair beside her and poured herself a cup of tea as well. This had become their morning ritual. Relaxing with a kettle of green tea in the garden before beginning her physical therapy or just taking a walk around the neighborhood.

"Sounds like it's getting pretty serious with your daddy and his friend," Mama Ellis said.

"I think it is. This is the first time we've all gone out to dinner rather than Karen or Daddy cooking at the house."

"I'm glad. I know he loved your mama, but it's about time for him to move on and live his life. I'm sure she wouldn't want him putting it on hold the way he has been," Mama Ellis said.

"I told him that after dinner. I like Karen and I think she's been good for him. He deserves to be happy," Belinda said.

"And what about you? Don't you deserve to be happy?" Mama Ellis asked.

"I am happy." Belinda picked an imaginary piece of lint off her top to avoid Mama Ellis's knowing gaze.

"You'd be happier if you and Eb would stop walking around trying not to notice each other and just admit how you feel," Mama Ellis said nonchalantly.

Belinda choked a little on the sip of tea she had just taken, and it took her a moment to recover. When she did she looked at Mama Ellis in surprise.

"Oh, don't look all shocked. You two have been making googly eyes at each other for weeks now. I may have had a stroke, but I'm not blind."

Belinda managed to recover from her surprise. "Ebony is my employer. I don't get involved with my clients or employers."

"Honey, when it comes to love, none of that matters. All that matters is that I've known Ebony since she was a little girl and after her daddy passed and her mama selfishly escaped into drugs and alcohol to numb the pain of her loss, I hadn't seen her at peace until I saw her looking at you just a week after I came home from the hospital. You said Karen is good for your daddy, well, you're good for our Eb, and I can tell by the way you look at her that you feel the same way about her." Mama Ellis stood. "Now, if you working for her is all that's in the way, then I'll gladly fire you because I can get another nurse easier than I can find another woman like you who will make my Eb happy," she said before heading back into the apartment.

Belinda sat in stunned silence for a moment then stood and picked up the tea service and headed toward the kitchen entrance of the private yard. Mama Ellis was wrong. What she and Ebony had for each other was physical attraction, not love. Belinda wasn't one of those people who believed in love at first sight. Love was something that grew over time, and she and Ebony barely had enough time to speak let alone develop emotional feelings for one another.

As she stood at the kitchen sink absentmindedly cleaning the teapot and cups they used, she thought of a moment several nights ago when they were all in the living room after dinner and she and Sheree were sitting on the floor playing Scrabble. She had looked up for just a moment and caught Ebony watching her. She'd grown used to seeing the heated sexual need in her eyes since the night they'd had sex, but that night there was something deeper. There was a look of such tender affection that Belinda had quickly looked away, not sure how to handle it.

A moment later, Mama Ellis announced she was going to bed, and after Belinda made sure she was okay and came back to the living room, Ebony was gone. She hadn't seen or spoken with her since that night until she'd called this morning to tell her she had to leave for the week.

No, she thought, it was purely sexual. It couldn't be love. It didn't matter that whenever Ebony walked into the room her heart skipped a beat and she felt like a silly schoolgirl crushing on the star athlete. It wasn't love when she took pleasure in preparing Ebony's favorites when she knew she'd be joining them for dinner or wanting to ease her stress when she noticed how tired she was after a long day at the studio.

After all, she took care of people for a living, why wouldn't she want to give comfort where she could? And for all she knew, Ebony could've been looking at Sheree the other night and she just happened to catch eye contact with her. No, Mama Ellis had to be mistaken. Belinda tried to convince herself, but the ache in her heart at not being able to see Ebony for a whole week told her otherwise.

Belinda distracted herself from thinking further about what Mama Ellis said by changing their therapy routine with a trip to the homeless shelter Mama Ellis had been so involved with before her stroke. It was the first time she'd been back, and although she still needed the cane for assistance to get around and tired out a little quicker than she used to, the staff adored her and found ways to involve her with activities.

Belinda enjoyed watching her reading stories to the little ones or helping the teenagers with their schoolwork when she could. It turned out Mama Ellis had been a school teacher for many years before she and her husband moved to Chicago from Ohio. She knew a break from the physical therapy and doing something with more challenging interaction to strengthen her mental capacity would be good for her. She also secretly hoped it would distract Mama Ellis from discussing her and Ebony further.

Midway through the week, Belinda lay in bed late one night reading, when her cell phone buzzed on the nightstand. To her surprise, it was Ebony.

After taking a deep breath to slow her racing heart, she answered. "Hello."

"Hey, it's Ebony."

"Hey, Ebony. How's your trip going?"

"It's good. How's Mama Ellis doing?"

"She's had a busy few days, but she's doing well."

"Yeah, Sheree told me you took her by the homeless shelter for a couple of days. She loves that place so I'm sure she had a good time."

"Yes, she did. It was good for her to get out and interact with the kids. If it's okay with you I'd like to make that a regular routine for her at least once or twice a week, depending on how she's feeling."

"Yeah, sure, if you feel like it's helping with her recovery then I'm fine with it. By the way, I don't think I've thanked you for the great work you're doing with Mama Ellis. She's recovering better than I expected."

"You're welcome, but I can't take all the credit. She's a determined woman. I think that as long as you had a good nurse she would've made the same progress because of her strong will to get better."

"Yeah, maybe."

They were both quiet for a moment.

Ebony cleared her throat, then said, "Well, I'll let you go. I'm sure you're tired."

"No, actually I couldn't sleep and was just reading." Belinda realized she missed the sound of Ebony's voice. She didn't want the call to end yet.

"Oh, anything good?"

"Just an article in the current issue of *Essence* about how to spice up your love life."

Ebony chuckled. "Does your love life need spicing up?"

"Kind of hard to spice up something that doesn't exist," Belinda answered.

"I can't imagine you not having someone at home making sure you're taken care of just as well as you take care of others," Ebony said.

Belinda felt her face heat with a blush. "My work keeps me too busy to focus on a relationship."

"So how do you unwind when you're not working?" Ebony asked.

"I spend time with my friends and my family," Belinda answered, wondering why Ebony was suddenly so interested in her personal life. They'd been pretty much living under the same roof for weeks now, and she had never once asked anything personal.

"What about you?" Belinda asked, turning the tables on her. "What do you do on the rare occasion you aren't working?"

"You already know the answer to that. If I'm not in the studio I'm usually down at Mama Ellis's," Ebony answered.

"And there's no one special in your life outside of Mama Ellis and Sheree?" Belinda asked.

Ebony was quiet for a moment, and Belinda's belly fluttered nervously waiting for her to answer.

"No," Ebony responded.

Belinda grew quiet once again. So much wanting to be said hanging in the silence.

Ebony was the first to speak. "So…uh…that first night… when we…"

"Had sex," Belinda quietly finished for her. If there was a time to finally discuss what happened she guessed now was as good a time as any.

"Yeah," Ebony said. "Thank you for not letting it get in the way of helping Mama Ellis."

"I take my job very seriously, Ebony. You and I signed a contract, and what happened between us had nothing to do with whether or not I could perform my job and fulfill that contract," Belinda said, a little annoyed that this is where that subject was leading rather than discussing why it happened.

"Yeah, well, a contract never stopped some women from taking advantage of my family," Ebony said coldly. "Hell, for all I know you could've been talking to a lawyer all this time trying to see what you can get."

"Wow, somebody must've really done a number on you," Belinda said.

"Excuse me?"

"You can't trust anybody can you? You can't imagine someone wanting to be with you just to be with you and not to get something from you. I feel sorry for you," Belinda said.

"You feel sorry for me?" Ebony said with an angry laugh. "You ain't got to feel sorry for me cuz I got everything I could possibly want or need."

"Do you?" Belinda asked.

"Yeah, I do," she said with a tremulous laugh.

"Well, if that's the case then you're better off than most of us." Belinda wondered how their friendly conversation had taken such an angry turn. "Look, I've got to get up early. I'll let Mama Ellis know you called to check up on her."

"Yeah, okay. Good night," Ebony said brusquely then hung up before Belinda could respond.

Belinda tossed her phone to the bottom of the bed in frustration and swore she was done with Ebony Trent. From this point on it was strictly business.

The week ended with no further calls from Ebony, and Belinda was actually relieved about it. She was in the guest room gathering her belongings to head home for the weekend when Sheree walked in.

"Hey, girl, I see you're packing up already. You're not going to stay and wait for Ebony to get home?" Sheree asked as she sat on the bed.

"No, I want to run a couple of errands before I go home and don't want to wait too late to do them," Belinda said, feeling guilty for lying to Sheree, but she just didn't want to be here when Ebony returned home.

"Okay, you'll just see her tomorrow," Sheree said matter-of-factly.

Confused, Belinda said, "Tomorrow? Tomorrow is Saturday, my day off."

"Yeah, it's also our belated welcome home dinner for Mama Ellis at Chayse's Place. Did you forget?" Sheree asked.

"No, I didn't even know about it," Belinda told her.

Sheree now had a look of confusion. "Ebony didn't call you this week to invite you?"

"She called, but she didn't mention the dinner," Belinda said.

"Did you two have a fight?"

Belinda went back to gathering her items. "It wasn't a fight. Your sister was just being her usual self."

Sheree sighed in frustration. "And you two were getting along so well."

"Yeah, but that's because she and I rarely interact. We have you and Mama Ellis as buffers," Belinda said.

"Well, you'll still come won't you? Mama Ellis would be heartbroken if she doesn't have all of her girls there," Sheree said hopefully.

"Sheree, I don't know. After this last conversation with Ebony I think I should really keep the socializing down to a minimum. Honestly, this is the most social interaction I've had with a client and their family. I've gotten really attached to you and Mama Ellis, which was not very professional of me," Belinda admitted.

Sheree stood, walked over to Belinda, and grasped her hands. "We've grown attached to you as well, which is why you have to come to the dinner. I'll make sure Ebony is on her best behavior."

"Ha! Good luck with that," Belinda said.

"Will you come?" Sheree asked with a sad puppy dog expression.

"How could I resist that face. All right, I'll be there."

❖

"You did what?!" Ebony loudly exclaimed, causing Sheree to flinch in response.

"Belinda said you hadn't invited her to tonight's dinner so I did," Sheree said.

"This dinner is just supposed to be family. Belinda's not family. She works for us," Ebony said in annoyance.

"You know Mama Ellis wants her there, she told you that herself, which was the reason you said you would call and invite her. But instead of doing that you call and pick a fight with her," Sheree said.

"I didn't pick a fight with her," Ebony pouted.

"Well, you said something because now she's feeling like she's broken some professional rule and allowed herself to become too close to her patient's family. She thinks she needs to keep it professional and not socialize with us the way she's been doing," Sheree explained.

Ebony looked away, not wanting Sheree to see the guilt in her eyes. "She said that?"

"Not in so many words, but it's basically how she feels. Look, Eb, the fact that she hasn't walked away after what happened that first night should show you she can be trusted. As much as I hate saying it, Mama Ellis won't live forever, and I would like to marry, have kids and a place of my own someday without worrying about who's going to remind you to eat when you're working in the studio for days on end, or pull you out of those dark moods you tend to fall into," Sheree said, her voice filled with emotion.

Ebony looked up to meet her sister's loving gaze. "I don't know what to say," she admitted.

Sheree reached across Ebony's kitchen counter and grasped her hands. "Say what's in your heart. You did it for years with your music. It's now time to practice what you preached."

Ebony grinned. "Guess that psychology class is paying off."

Sheree chuckled. "Gotta show you all your hard earned money isn't going to waste."

"You know I love you, right," Ebony said, suddenly serious once again.

"Yes, and hopefully tonight you'll be able to tell Belinda the same thing," Sheree said.

❖

Ebony glanced nervously toward the doorway that led out to Chayse's Place garden dining area where she, Sheree, and Mama Ellis had just been seated moments earlier.

"Anyone ever tell you a watched pot never boils?" Mama Ellis said with a knowing grin.

Ebony sent a frustrated glance toward Sheree.

"I didn't say a word," Sheree said.

"She didn't have to. I'd have to be blind not to notice the way you too are always watching each other when you think no one's looking," Mama Ellis told Ebony.

"Don't you two have anything better to do than watching me?" Ebony looked down at her glass of wine, only mildly annoyed.

Mama Ellis and Sheree just grinned in response as it only took a moment for Ebony's gaze to drift back toward the doorway. This time it was met by Chayse's who was smiling broadly as she led Belinda by the hand to their table.

"Well, look who I found wandering in," Chayse said.

Ebony found she couldn't speak. One reason was the spike of jealousy she felt at seeing Chayse holding Belinda's hand. The other was because Belinda didn't look like the Belinda she knew. Instead of her usual entwined bun, Belinda's locs were flowing freely down her back in a curly style. She wore gold and turquoise dangle earrings with a matching necklace, a sleeveless burnt orange knee-length wrap dress that molded to her luscious curves and complemented her smooth dark skin, and a pair of sexy gold strappy heels that showed off her French manicured toes. Ebony hadn't seen Belinda in anything other than her nurse uniform since they first met, so to see her in regular clothes looking sexy as hell caught her off guard.

Ebony watched as Belinda greeted first Sheree and Mama Ellis with an affection hug and then turned a wary gaze toward her.

"Hello, Ebony," Belinda said coolly.

"Hey," and a head nod was all Ebony could muster in response.

Belinda's gaze stayed with hers for just a moment before she turned back toward Chayse.

"Did you get my message earlier?" Belinda asked Chayse.

"Yeah, I got you, girl. Don't worry about a thing," Chayse said with a conspiratorial wink.

"Thanks," Belinda said with a sweet smile before placing a soft kiss on Chayse's cheek.

Ebony could see the affection they held for one another in their expressions, especially Chayse's, and her mood darkened watching their interaction.

After Chayse assisted with Belinda's chair she announced, "Mama Ellis, in honor of your comeback, and gracing Chayse's Place with your beauty and wisdom, dinner tonight is on the house."

"You don't have to do that," Ebony said.

"I know but I want to," Chayse said. "Your appetizers will be out in a moment. Belinda, you having your usual?"

"Yes, thanks, Chayse," Belinda answered.

Chayse nodded and walked away.

"Belinda, you are working that dress, isn't she, Mama Ellis," Sheree said.

"Yes, she is. It's so nice to see you out of that uniform. Thank you for coming, honey," Mama Ellis said.

"I wouldn't miss it for the world," Belinda said, grasping Mama Ellis's hand.

As she, Mama Ellis, and Sheree chatted about a possible shopping expedition to one of the outlet malls, Belinda found it difficult to focus. She could feel Ebony's heated gaze on her, and she fought not to turn toward her. When she walked out and saw Ebony looking as fine as ever, she didn't think she would have been able to walk if Chayse hadn't been holding her hand. With a fresh haircut, Ebony was wearing large diamond stud earrings, a simple gold chain around her neck, stonewashed jeans that fit loose but not loose enough to hide her firm behind, black suede Timberland boots, and an untucked white button-down shirt under a black suede blazer with the shirt and blazer sleeves both rolled over her forearms showing the three meditation bead bracelets Belinda had never seen her without. To Belinda, she was sexy no matter what she wore, but there seemed to be a darkness to the sex appeal she was feeling from Ebony tonight and it thrilled and frightened her all at once.

Ebony barely spoke throughout the dinner, picking over her food with a dark, brooding countenance. Mama Ellis and Sheree simply ignored her, but Belinda could feel Ebony's mood moving around them like the chill in the air right before a thunderstorm. At one point during dessert she pulled her wrap out of her bag and wrapped it around her shoulders for warmth.

Ebony asked, "Are you cold?" with an angry frown.

"A little," Belinda answered hesitantly.

To Belinda's surprise, Ebony stood, took her blazer off, and walked around her chair to lay it across her shoulders. Mama Ellis and Sheree stopped in mid conversation to watch in awed silence.

"Thank you," Belinda said.

"Welcome," Ebony said, beginning to relax for the first time that night.

The mood was quickly broken by Chayse's arrival.

"Sorry to disturb you folks, but, Belinda, she's here," Chayse said, not looking pleased.

Belinda frowned as well. "She's early."

"You want me to have her wait?" Chayse asked.

Belinda sighed. "No, I'll be right there. Thanks, Chayse."

Chayse nodded and walked away.

Belinda stood. "I'm sorry to leave a little early, but I promised to meet someone tonight after our dinner and it looks like she's here early. Thank you for inviting me," Belinda said as she gave Mama Ellis and Sheree a hug and kiss in departing.

When she reached Ebony she said, "Thank you again," and handed her jacket back to her, already missing the warm musk scent of Ebony's cologne that had enveloped her when she had placed it over her shoulders.

Their hands brushed in the exchange, and Ebony's gaze met hers with such longing that Belinda's heart seemed to skip a beat. Ebony looked as if she were about to speak, then suddenly changed her mind.

Ebony turned away. "Guess we'll see you on Monday," she said as she put her jacket back on.

Belinda turned to say good-bye once again to Sheree and Mama Ellis and saw both of them looking at Ebony in frustration. Wanting to avoid getting in any deeper emotionally than she was with this odd little family, Belinda just turned and made her way into the restaurant. She walked to the end of the bar where her ex-girlfriend, Carla, waited.

Ebony sat nursing a now warm beer as she watched the two women talking and wondered what the hell she was doing. She had sent Sheree and Mama Ellis home with the excuse that she had to go into the studio. As soon as she put them in the car that was waiting for them she went right back into Chayse's and found a table in a dark corner that would allow her to see and not be seen by Belinda as she watched her. She realized how crazy she was probably acting but couldn't bring herself to leave. Sheree had told Ebony, not that she hadn't realized it herself, that she had blown the perfect opportunity to tell Belinda how she felt.

Ebony knew it was fear that had held her tongue. Fear that Belinda didn't feel the same way and that she'd be left feeling like a fool once again. The same way she had felt when her mother had come back into their lives a year after Ebony had moved them to New York. She had sworn she changed and hoped Ebony would give her a chance to make up for leaving them the way she did. Ebony had been wary, but Mama Ellis suggested she give her a chance, and Sheree had been so happy to have her mother back in her life, so she let her into their circle.

Everything had been fine for almost a year. Her mother stayed close to home, not wanting to be in the limelight. When people asked Ebony who she was she'd say her mother was a family member she was helping out for a while. And just when Ebony was getting comfortable with the thought of her family being together again, just when she let her guard down, she came home after picking up Sheree from school to find Mama Ellis handcuffed to the bathroom sink, their home trashed, and their mother, as well as anything worth value, gone.

It turned out that their mother had used her connection to them to gain their trust so that she could help her pimp, drug-dealing boyfriend to rob Ebony blind. Ebony found out all this when she used some of her not so legal connections from her old life to find her mother and boyfriend. She gave instructions that she didn't care what happened to the boyfriend and his crew, but she wanted her mother unharmed and brought to her.

Unbeknownst to Mama Ellis and Sheree, Ebony had flown to Chicago, confronted her mother, and told her that if she ever came seeking her out again she would personally put her out of her crack addict misery. They never heard from their mother again, and Ebony never let anyone past the fortress she had erected around her heart again. Until now, she thought as she watched Belinda laugh at something the woman she was with said.

"You know, most people would consider this stalking," Chayse said as she sat in the chair beside Ebony.

"Mind your business, Chayse," Ebony said threateningly.

"Look, Ebony, you're my boi. I'm just trying to look out for you," Chayse said, her tone suddenly serious.

"You sure that's all it is?"

"Ebony, you know me. I'm not about competing for a woman. Especially one that's into somebody else," Chayse answered.

Ebony's gaze slid from Chayse's back toward Belinda and her friend. "So is that who she's into?"

Chayse followed Ebony's gaze and grinned knowingly. "Ebony, that's not—"

Chayse's comment was cut short when Ebony quickly stood and started making her way toward Belinda. Belinda and her companion were in a quiet but heated conversation as Belinda tried to unsuccessfully pull her wrist from the other woman's grasp. Ebony was already at Belinda's side before Chayse was half way there.

"Are you all right, Belinda?" Ebony asked.

Belinda looked up at Ebony in surprise. "Ebony? I thought you all left a while ago?"

"Mama Ellis and Sheree did. I stayed. Are you all right?" Ebony asked again, her voice taking on an angry growl as she lowered her gaze toward Belinda's still grasped wrist.

Belinda quickly snatched her arm away. "I'm fine," she said unconvincingly.

"Who the hell are you?" her companion asked as she stood to address Ebony.

Ebony slowly turned toward the other woman.

Belinda looked on worriedly. "Carla, this is my employer, Ebony Trent."

Carla had a height advantage over Ebony, but Ebony had bulk and muscle over Carla's slim frame.

Carla frowned in confusion for a moment, then her eyes lit up with recognition. "Hold up, Ebony Trent as in Ebony 'The Beast' Trent?" she asked with a huge grin. "Yo, you didn't tell me you worked for The Beast," Carla said to Belinda.

She held out a hand toward Ebony. "I'm a big fan."

Ebony ignored Carla and turned back toward Belinda. "You didn't look all right."

"I said I was fine…wait, were you watching me?" Belinda asked.

Carla's chuckling stopped Ebony from answering. "Now I see why you haven't been returning my calls. You been sleeping with the boss, and seeing who it is, I wouldn't blame you."

Ebony turned, fists clinched at her sides, and said in a low growl, "Walk away right now."

The grin slid from Carla's face into a worried frown. "You don't have to ask me twice."

She slowly slid past Ebony, gave Belinda a quick nod in parting, and walked away.

When Ebony turned around, Belinda was wrapping her shawl around her shoulders and turning to leave.

"Where are you going?" Ebony asked in confusion.

"Anywhere you aren't," Belinda said angrily.

Ebony watched her walk away.

"You're going to have to work on that charm of yours," Chayse said.

Ebony lowered her head, sighing in frustration. "I don't know why I seem to act like such a complete ass around her."

"I think you're really feeling something for her you've never felt before and don't know how to handle it."

Ebony gazed up at her. "So what do I do about it?"

"Go after her. Talk to her. Tell her how you feel," Chayse advised.

"Yeah, she's really gonna listen to me after I just broke up her date."

"Ebony, that wasn't a date. Carla is her ex."

"Her ex? She looking to get back with her?"

"Hell no. Carla runs through women like a junkie runs through needles. She's only trying to get Belinda back because she was the only one who refused to put up with Carla's bullshit. She was dumped by Belinda before she could do the dumping."

Ebony couldn't help but think that sounded very much how she had been treating women for as long as she could remember.

"You two are nothing alike," Chayse said, as if reading Ebony's thoughts. "Carla has no heart. She gets bored and moves on. You on the other hand have a heart hidden behind a protective wall and push women away when they get too close to keep your heart from being broken. Ebony, Belinda's not your mother or any of those other shallow women you've dated. She's not out to get anything from you. You want something with somebody genuine, Belinda is your woman. Go after her before you completely blow any chance of experiencing what a relationship with a real woman can do for you."

An hour later, Ebony was standing outside Belinda's apartment building in Brooklyn. She didn't quite know what to expect, but she definitely didn't expect to find her living at The Boerum, luxury condos in Boerum Hill. Ebony had looked at purchasing one of these condos a year ago but didn't because she liked the way the brownstone in Harlem allowed them to all have their own apartments, something they wouldn't have had living in a condominium. She knew Belinda was paid well, but she didn't think it was well enough to live in a two-million-dollar condo.

"Hi, can I help you?" the concierge in the lobby asked.

"Uh, yeah. I'm Ebony Trent, here to see Belinda Jansen," Ebony said.

He nodded then picked up the phone and called up to Belinda. "Ms. Jansen, there's a Ms. Trent here to see you."

Belinda must have gone quiet on the other end because the doorman said, "Ms. Jansen, you there?" He listened for a moment then said, "Yes, ma'am. You can go up," he told Ebony.

"Thanks," Ebony said then walked to the elevator, her mind racing with what to say. She hadn't thought it out this far because she honestly thought Belinda wouldn't want to see her. Once she reached Belinda's door, she took a deep breath and knocked.

Belinda opened the door and, without a word, stepped aside to allow Ebony to enter. Ebony could tell by the long foyer that this was one of the three-bedroom condos she had looked at. Maybe Belinda had roommates and that's how she could afford living there. It had modern but comfortable furnishing with warm wood and earth tone decor. Ebony closed her eyes and breathed in the scent of lavender mingled with Belinda's own subtle scent and began to feel as if all the tension she'd held for so long was slowly drifting from her body.

"Why are you here, Ebony?" Belinda asked.

Ebony slowly opened her eyes to find Belinda standing in front of her, arms crossed and looking very annoyed.

"I came to see if you're okay," Ebony said.

"You could've picked up the phone to do that," Belinda said.

"Can we talk?"

Belinda stood there for a moment, holding Ebony's gaze, as if trying to figure her out then shrugged in resignation. "Come sit down." She led Ebony to the living room.

Ebony sat on the sofa and Belinda sat in a chair across from her with her knees tucked under her. It was the first time she noticed what Belinda was wearing, a long sleek animal print satin nightgown and a black robe, with the same animal print on the cuffs, belted at the waist. Her long locs were pulled up into a high ponytail and her smooth feet were bare. She was, as usual, sexy as hell and sent Ebony's mind into a place she was trying to avoid. Belinda watched her, waiting patiently for her to speak. Ebony cleared her throat, opened her mouth to speak but couldn't think of what to say first.

Belinda chose to speak instead. "Ebony, I can't keep working for you if every conversation we have is going to turn into a confrontation."

"What do you mean?" Ebony asked.

"After what happened tonight I think you should find another nurse for Mama Ellis. I'll be happy to refer two very good nurses who I know are available and are also very discreet. They're older and will probably be better company for Mama Ellis anyway," Belinda said.

"You're quitting?" Ebony said in surprise.

"Yes. I'll finish out the week to give you time to interview my replacement," Belinda said.

"You can't quit," Ebony said in frustration.

"I also can't keep walking on eggshells worried about what will be the next thing I'll say or do to set you off. I don't know if it's because of what happened my first night at Mama Ellis's or if it's just simply the fact that you and I will never get along, but whatever it is it makes being there unbearable."

"I...Mama Ellis...needs you," Ebony said hesitantly.

Belinda gazed at Ebony questioningly, not sure if she heard Ebony correctly or if it was just a mistake. Either way, she chose to ignore it.

"The difficult part of her care and physical therapy is over and she honestly doesn't require full-time assistance any longer. She's as close to being her old self-sufficient self as she ever will be. I've already spoken to my father about her progress, and he agrees with my recommendation of hiring a part-time physical therapist to continue to work with her a couple of times of week," Belinda said.

Ebony frowned. "So that's it?"

"Yes. I'll let Mama Ellis know when I see her on Monday," Belinda said with a sad smile.

Ebony nodded then stood and head for the door without a word. Belinda was so used to Ebony's sudden departures when she didn't want to deal with something that she didn't try to stop her. What would be the point? Belinda sat for a few moments in the silence that followed wondering if the sadness and sense of loss she felt was because of the unexpected attachment she had formed with Mama Ellis and Sheree, or in spite of how much she had tried to avoid it, she had developed deeper feelings for Ebony than she wanted to admit.

As she thought back over the past several weeks, she realized that Ebony's unpredictable mood swings had come fewer and farther between the more times they all spent together. Although she and Ebony rarely spent time alone, or even had full conversations when they were together with Mama Ellis and Sheree, Belinda felt such peace and comfort at knowing Ebony was there. The physical attraction was still there, but over time other feelings had developed in those shared moments with the Trent family. Unfortunately, judging by Ebony's attitude toward her, the feeling was obviously not mutual.

"Well, after next week, none of that will matter," Belinda said out loud as she stood and began turning out the lights on her way to bed, which was where she was headed when Ebony arrived.

Just as Belinda reached her bedroom, there was a knock at her apartment door. The only person who would be over this late was her neighbor Phyllis who sometimes dropped in on her with a bottle of wine when her boyfriend pissed her off.

"Phyllis, you really need to learn to call first," Belinda said with a laugh as she opened the door.

To her surprise, it was Ebony who closed the short distance between them in one quick step, gently grasped Belinda's face with both hands, and kissed her so deeply, so passionately, that it left her senseless. Ebony slowly broke the kiss but didn't release Belinda's face. She softly stroked her cheek with the pad of her thumb as she once again gazed into Belinda's eyes with such a vulnerable expression it made Belinda's heart ache.

Belinda grasped one of Ebony's hands, pulled her fully into the apartment, closed the door, and led Ebony to her bedroom. Belinda was tired of fighting. Tired of second-guessing why she was so strongly drawn to Ebony. She threw caution to the wind, allowing her heart to lead the way.

When they reached Belinda's bedroom she turned back toward Ebony and began undressing her. She unbuttoned Ebony's shirt and slowly slid both her shirt and blazer off her shoulders and down her arms, laying them on a chair nearby. She pulled the tank top she wore out of the waistband of her jeans, running her hands smoothly up along Ebony's rib cage as she pulled it up her torso and over her head. Ebony's eyes closed and her head fell back in reaction to Belinda's touch.

Belinda allowed her gaze to wander over Ebony's body, enjoying how sexy she looked in her black sports bra above her six-pack abs, her jeans that rode low on her hips, showing off the waistband of her designer briefs and round behind. When she looked up, she met Ebony's passion-darkened eyes, and she shivered with desire in response. Belinda kept her eyes locked with Ebony's as she reached down to unbutton the fly of Ebony's jeans, slip her thumbs into the waistband, and slide them down her legs, going to her knees before Ebony. Balancing on the back of the chair nearby, Ebony lifted one leg and then the other so that Belinda could remove her shoes and pants completely.

Belinda ran her hands up the length of Ebony's muscular legs, massaging from her ankles to where the cuff of her briefs began. She knelt within eye level of Ebony's torso and leaned forward to press hot kisses to the bare flesh along the waistband of Ebony's briefs.

To see Belinda kneeling before her, to feel her soft lips pressed against her sensitive skin, had Ebony barely holding on to the self-control she was trying so hard to maintain. With a shuddering sigh, she closed her eyes, balling her hands into tight fists and pressing her nails into her palms to stay focused. But it seemed Belinda had other ideas in mind when she hooked her thumbs into the waistband of her briefs, slid them down her legs, made Ebony lift her feet again to remove them, and then ran her hands up the length of her legs to cup her behind. When Ebony felt Belinda's warm breath on her belly followed by the tip of her tongue tracing a hot trail along the juncture of her thighs, she had to grab hold of the chair to keep from falling over.

Ebony adjusted her stance a little wider, giving Belinda the incentive to continue. She delved her tongue in the upper area of Ebony's pussy lips to stroke it along her clit. Ebony moaned deeply as Belinda expertly sucked and stroked the enlarged nub with her lips and tongue, surprising her by how quickly Belinda was bringing her to the peak of ecstasy. Ebony's grip tightened and her legs threatened to buckle beneath her as her passion built. Just when she thought she couldn't hold back anymore, Belinda halted her lusty ministrations and stood. Ebony closed her eyes and gritted her teeth trying to steady her racing heart and pulsing womanhood.

Belinda grazed her lips across Ebony's, up to her ear, and whispered, "What do you want, Ebony?"

Ebony found it hard to think, let alone speak. She opened her eyes and met Belinda's passion-glazed, questioning gaze. She was standing there, ass out, as turned on as she could possibly be and this woman was asking her what she wanted?

As if reading her thoughts, Belinda said, "If all you want is an uncomplicated fuck buddy, then I'm not the one and you can get dressed and leave right now. But if you want more, if you want a real woman who doesn't give a damn about what's in your bank account, because frankly, as you can see from my home, I don't need it, a woman who will respect you, beast and all, a woman who will share your life, not run it or be run by it, then stay. The choice is yours."

Ebony saw the raw sincerity in Belinda's eyes and felt such a tightness in her chest she almost couldn't breathe. "I...I..." she stammered to find the words.

"You what, Ebony?" Belinda asked gently.

Ebony's hands clenched into fists, anger hardened her face, and she roared in frustration. This was The Beast, this was the darkness that came out in Ebony's music. Ebony's body trembled and every muscle in her body seemed ready to snap at any moment.

"I'm not afraid of you," Belinda said.

"Why? Maybe you should be," Ebony practically growled.

"Because I've met the real you. I've met the gentle, loving, protective you." Belinda raised Ebony's clenched fists and placed a gentle kiss on each one. "I've also met this Ebony, The Beast, the survivor, and I don't fear her because I admire her. I admire her strength and her passion. This Ebony is the one who did what it took to make something of herself, to give her family a better life than the one she knew. This Ebony is the one who will do whatever it takes to protect those she loves even if it means she has to sacrifice her own happiness to do so."

Ebony gazed down at her hard, large fists enveloped in the soft, warm grasp of Belinda's hands and felt the tightness in her chest loosen a bit. She gazed up into the understanding in Belinda's eyes and it loosened even more. She took a deep, shuddering breath and felt tension begin to ease from her taut muscles. In spite of all of that, her beast still held, waiting, and Ebony knew what it wanted. It wanted her to walk out right now because Belinda would be like all the rest, a user until she got what she wanted and left Ebony with her heart cold and dead. Just like her mother. But looking at Belinda, seeing now for the first time that there was not just understanding but love in her eyes, Ebony ignored her beast and listened to her heart.

"I want you...I need you...to show me how to love again," she said quietly.

Belinda released Ebony's fists and gently grasped her face.

"You already know how to love, Ebony, you just have to let others love you back," Belinda said. "Let me love you, Ebony."

"I don't know if I can," Ebony said, feeling that tightness once again.

"You can if you just let go. All that pain and anger inside is what's holding you back. It's time to let go of that abandoned and lost little girl and embrace the strong, loving woman she's become," Belinda said, wiping a tear from Ebony's cheek.

Until that moment Ebony hadn't even realized she was crying. What the hell? Ebony Trent doesn't cry, she thought to herself. She hadn't cried since the day she realized her mother wasn't coming back and she and Sheree were on their own. The memory of that day, and all the hardships and struggles that followed, brought forward all the pain she only allowed to be released when she wrote her lyrics, but this time she had no pen or paper to write. She stood there literally naked and bare in front of the only other person besides Sheree and Mama Ellis that she loved.

She could no longer fight it, she loved Belinda, and to see the love and concern reflected back to her from Belinda's deep brown eyes was her undoing. The pressure in Ebony's chest broke like a dam that could no longer hold back a raging river. She staggered back against the chair in surprise at the wash of emotion that ran through her. Her legs gave out and she slid to the floor at Belinda's feet, her eyes filling with tears and a painful moan escaping from her lips.

Belinda quickly knelt before her. "Ebony?" she said in concern, while pulling her into her arms.

Ebony tensed for a moment, not used to being comforted. It felt so right to be in Belinda's arms, and she could no longer fight the emotions overwhelming her. Belinda held her tighter as Ebony's body shook with heartrending sobs. She wept for the innocence lost when she and Sheree were abandoned and she was forced to grow up too fast, having to do things to survive that shamed her just to think about them. She wept for the angry woman she'd become, sometimes even shutting out those closest to her just to avoid feeling too much or making herself vulnerable to being hurt.

As her weeping slowly subsided, she not only felt drained but also as if something physically shifted within her. As she lay quietly in Belinda's arms, her head resting on the fullness of her breasts, listening to the comforting rhythm of her heartbeat, Ebony realized what it was, she no longer felt the heavy darkness in her heart that she'd worn like a badge of honor for the past sixteen years. It had been replaced by a warmth and a lightness that gave her a sense of emotional freedom that she had never known before.

"Are you okay?" Belinda asked.

Ebony nodded, at a loss for words as she gazed up at Belinda, this amazing woman who, like some heroine in a fairy tale, broke the dark spell Belinda had been under for so long.

She knelt in front of Belinda, gently took her face within her hands, locked her gaze with Belinda, and with all the emotion she felt in her heart told her, "I love you."

Tears gathered and glistened in Belinda's eyes. "I know," Belinda said with a soft smile.

Ebony laughed out loud. A rich, joyous laugh.

"What am I going to do with you?" Ebony said.

"I can think of a few things," Belinda said.

"Really?" Ebony said in that seductively low tone that made Belinda's body flush with heat.

Ebony then brought Belinda's face toward hers and kissed her slowly, passionately, thoroughly. When their lips parted, Ebony grasped her hand and stood, leading Belinda to her bed. Once there she removed Belinda's robe and nightgown then laid her on the bed. Belinda shivered with anticipation as she saw Ebony's eyes darken with passion and her lips curve into a seductive grin in a look that told her that her love may have tamed the beast but it still crouched in the darkness, waiting for moments like this to stalk forward and appease its insatiable appetite. Belinda was thrilled to be its willing prey, for that night and many nights to come...mind, body, and heart.

AWAKEN

Based on the Sleeping Beauty *fairy tale*

Chayse Carmichael dipped a spoon in the industrial sized pot simmering on one of the three large stoves in the Chayse's Place kitchen to taste the contents.

"Nikko, you forgot the whiskey," she said to the sous chef in training standing beside her.

"Whiskey, Chef? In collard greens? I've never heard of such a thing," Nikko said in disgust.

The usually loud, boisterous kitchen went silent and all eyes turned toward Chayse, everyone waiting for the sparks to fly. Chayse sighed, handed the spoon she had used to a bus boy standing nearby, and turned slowly toward the young man looking arrogantly down his nose at her. She'd worked too long and too hard to get where she was today to have some twenty-year-old snot-nosed wannabe bratty son of a celebrity chef tell her how to run her own kitchen. Chayse took Nikko under her wing three weeks ago as a favor to his father, a well-known Italian cuisine chef she had studied under when she was first starting out. He had called her to ask if she would mentor his son, and she couldn't possibly say no to one of her own mentors.

When he told her Nikko could be a bit of a handful she hadn't thought anything of it until his second day in her kitchen when he took it upon himself to make a change to her fried okra recipe by eliminating the corn meal, using just flour, and exchanging buttermilk for regular milk because he thought both made it too heavy. She hadn't found out until a few of her regulars that night asked her why she changed the recipe. She had calmly explained to Nikko that although he was welcome to make suggestions he was not allowed to make changes without speaking with her first.

He had ignored her and attempted to make other changes the following week, but her other two chefs had circumvented the dishes before they made it out onto the floor. From that point on he was not allowed to prepare any of the dishes going out; he was simply there to learn how to prepare them from her and her other chefs. He had spent this last week criticizing under his breath how she ran her kitchen and, frankly, she was tired of it.

"Get out of my kitchen," she said calmly, trying to keep her temper in check.

"Excuse me?" Nikko said in confusion.

"I said get out of my kitchen," she repeated.

"You cannot just kick me out like I'm some common fry cook," Nikko said indignantly.

"Man, you are really testing my patience," Chayse said. "That's my name on the restaurant, my money that pays the bills, and my food that everyone is eating so I can do anything I damn well please. Now, get the hell out of my kitchen… my restaurant…before they have to take you out of here on a stretcher."

Nikko opened his mouth to speak, then, with an indignant huff, he gathered his personal chef knives and headed for the door.

"I will be informing my father of this," he said.

Chayse waved him away dismissively. "Give him my regards."

After Nikko stomped his way out of the kitchen, she turned back to her staff. "Show is over, ladies and gents, get back to work. Doors open in thirty minutes."

As Chayse went about her routine of preparing the restaurant for the Sunday brunch crowd, she thought back to all those years ago standing on a chair in her grandmother's kitchen helping her prepare Sunday dinner for the family. That was where she fell in love with cooking at the tender age of five, and by the time she was twelve she could prepare a three-course meal by herself. Her parents encouraged her talent and beamed with pride when she graduated from culinary school and then decided to continue her studies in Europe.

As a going away gift, her grandmother had collected all of the family recipes and given them to Chayse's sister who had them printed into a spiral bound cookbook for her. That cookbook became Chayse's bible. It went wherever she did, and when she decided to open her own restaurant she knew the menu would be based on the recipes from that book. She had even thought to name it Bea's Place, but her grandmother had put a stop to that real quick, saying she would feel foolish walking around with her name on a restaurant. So Chayse did the next best thing and put her own name on it.

Unfortunately, opening her own place wasn't as easy as she thought. Debt from her student loans kept her from getting a business loan, and investors didn't want to back an unknown in a soul food restaurant when there were already so many in New York. Her grandmother gave her the idea to get into catering, so she started catering small parties and events for her network of friends. Her business grew through word of mouth and referrals, but it wasn't until she and hip-hop artist Ebony "The Beast" Trent met and became friends that her dream for opening her own restaurant came to be.

Ebony was looking for an investment, and after seeing how well Chayse's catering business was doing she thought Chayse would be the perfect investment opportunity. With Ebony's backing, Chayse threw herself into making the restaurant a success. Sacrificing her personal life, and sometimes her sanity, to prove that it wasn't just another soul food spot. Ebony's contacts in the entertainment industry didn't hurt either. As soon as celebrities were spotted eating at Chayse's Place, business boomed, especially when regular folks realized that they could eat at the same place as their favorite entertainer without spending an arm and a leg to do so. There were two major stipulations Ebony made to Chayse—keep the food good and the prices reasonable, both of which Chayse had no issue with doing. That was six years ago, and Chayse had lines out the door most weekends and people making reservations months in advance just to ensure they got a seat.

One weekly reservation that caught Chayse's eye had been walking through the door like clockwork every Sunday for the past month. Serena, a stunning, thick sista with curves in all the right places, rich, golden brown complexion, a mane of thick, reddish brown natural curls that haloed her face and cascaded to just past her shoulders, hypnotic hazel eyes surrounded by long, thick lashes, and a softly upturned nose above full, sensual lips. Chayse always made it a point to be out in the dining area whenever Serena arrived. Taking the time to admire Serena's slow, easy grace as she walked across the room.

Other than smiles of greeting and quick, passing glances, Serena and Chayse had only spoken twice. The first was when Serena had asked the waiter if there was any way she could have one of Chayse's sweet potato pies shipped to her grandmother in Georgia. Chayse had come out to personally make sure the pie was shipped by the end of the week. She had made the pie herself the very next day instead of using one of the pre-made and frozen pies her pastry chef prepared, and then shipped it herself. The second time was last Sunday when she came in to thank Chayse and to give her a message from her grandmother. The joy on Serena's face when she talked about her grandmother reminded Chayse of how she felt about her own grandmother. It was one more of the growing number of reasons Chayse felt herself drawn to Serena.

Other than her name, the fact that Serena moved to New York from Georgia just six months ago for a job opportunity, and that she adored her grandmother, Chayse knew nothing else about the woman she had developed a serious attraction to. Today, Chayse planned to change that by stopping by Serena's table to ask about her grandmother in the hope of drawing her into a conversation about herself. The goal was to find out if, one, she was gay, and two, if she would go out with her. If the first answer was a no, then Chayse would walk away with her tail between her legs and go back to her other life partner, her cat, Lucky, and resign herself to being a bachelorette for the rest of her life.

When Serena was a no-show for that Sunday, Chayse was actually a little relieved. It turned out her dedication to her career left her more confident in the kitchen than with charming the ladies. Maybe Serena's new life in New York had finally brought her other interests to occupy her Sundays, she thought to herself as she locked up that night and made her way up to her loft apartment above the restaurant.

"Guess it's just you and me, huh, Lucky," she said to the black cat that met her at the door.

Lucky meowed in response as she wove herself through Chayse's legs. Chayse dropped her backpack by the door, bent down to pick up the cat, and headed into the kitchen. The loft took up the entire top floor above the restaurant and was laid out in an open floor plan with sliding doors that separated the master bedroom and bath from the main living space. Her kitchen area took a large portion of the farthest side of the space and was a home chef's dream kitchen. Chayse entertained family, friends, and business associates often, and a good kitchen was at the top of her list when she discussed the layout of the space with the architect.

She set Lucky on one of the stools along the kitchen island, turned on the TV, and prepared her four-legged roommate's dinner of leftover broiled tuna. Just as she was about to set Lucky's bowl down, a news story caught her attention. The reporter was saying that police were still looking for the identity of a woman who had been attacked while jogging in Riverside Park a few days ago. She was found unconscious with no identification and still remained in a coma at Harlem Hospital Center. When they showed the victim's picture asking if anyone could help identify her, Chayse's legs felt like they would collapse from under her and she had to grab the counter for support. It was Serena.

When Serena Frazier arrived in New York six months ago, it wasn't as a naïve, wide-eyed, fresh-faced dreamer entranced by the big lights of New York City. At thirty-four years old, she came focused, armed, and prepared to make a name for herself. At fourteen, she had started her own side hustle designing flyers, posters, websites, and even CD covers for small local clubs, businesses, concert promoters, and independent artists in and around her home of Savannah, Georgia, to help her parents save money for college. She graduated with a bachelor of fine arts in graphic design from Georgia Southern University and had spent the past twelve years clawing her way to a senior designer level at companies that couldn't see past her being a Black woman.

When an industry networking event put her in contact with Dennis Sanders, the CEO of a Black-owned graphic design start-up in New York, she couldn't pass up the opportunity to discuss her experience and ask for advice. They met for lunch the following day at the airport before his flight back to New

York, and two weeks later, he had called to offer her a creative director position at his firm.

Serena was thrilled. Her girlfriend of almost two years, Mel, wasn't. She couldn't believe Serena was seriously considering leaving just as they were starting to look at apartments together. As much as she cared about Mel, Serena knew that to pass up the opportunity to not only further her career but to work for Dennis Sanders, a designer whose work she had always admired, would be crazy. Mel didn't understand why Serena had to go all the way to New York when Raleigh, North Carolina, the Silicon Valley of the South, was practically next door. Serena felt that if Mel couldn't understand what such a step in her career would mean to her, then she really didn't know her at all. They argued for days until Serena finally broke it off with Mel. Within a day of that, Serena gave her notice at her job, called her cousin Alex who lived in Harlem to make arrangements to stay with her until she could find her own place, and within a month, said a tear-filled good-bye to her parents, brothers, and beloved grandmother and headed to New York.

Serena's first couple of months were a whirlwind with getting to know her role and her team as well as her new home city. Her cousin Alex traveled a lot for her job so Serena was left to fend for herself quite often. She had only visited New York a few times since her cousin moved up several years ago, and she always loved the loud, frenetic personality of the city. It fed her creativity, but visiting and living in it were two different things. When a bout of homesickness hit her, she questioned her decision.

To cheer her up, Alex took her to brunch at Chayse's Place one Sunday, which had the opposite effect she wanted. The food was so good it made her even more homesick for Sunday dinners at her grandmother's house. When Serena called her grandmother that night and told her she had made a mistake and was considering coming back home, her grandmother surprised her by telling her that would be the mistake. She reminded Serena how miserable she was working for people who didn't see her potential and appreciate her talent. It made no sense to work as long and as hard as she had to get where she was only to take a huge step backward because she missed her family.

"Child, we'll always be here. We aren't going anywhere anytime soon so wipe away that sadness and get back to doing you!" Serena's grandmother had told her.

Serena adored her grandmother's no-nonsense attitude. It was one of the main reasons she had called her instead of her mother because she knew her mother would agree that maybe she should come home. She had not been happy about Serena moving to New York in the first place, but her grandmother, father, and brothers had agreed it would be good for her to step out on her own. Because her mother seemed to be outnumbered, she gave up trying to convince Serena to stay in Georgia.

Taking her grandmother's advice to heart, Serena wiped away her sadness and found other activities that would focus on her other passions to occupy her time. She signed up for a community art class and joined a running club. She also decided to go back to Chayse's Place for Sunday brunch, but it would be at the same time her family usually had Sunday dinner so that she could at least get some down home food even if she couldn't be down home to have it.

That was when she got her first look at the restaurant's proprietor, Chayse Carmichael. Serena was usually attracted to feminine women, but there was something about Chayse's androgynous appearance, neither specifically feminine nor masculine, that drew her. She stood about five ten with a slim but muscular physique; loose, shoulder-length jet-black locs; smooth chocolate complexion; sleepy, light brown eyes; wide nose; and full lips that always seemed to be spread into a warm smile no matter who she spoke with. Serena had surreptitiously watched Chayse move through the restaurant, greeting guests and talking with staff here and there, and she secretly hoped Chayse would stop by her table as well. When their gazes caught for just a moment and Chayse's smile broadened a bit, Serena felt her heart flutter.

It seemed as if Chayse was going to make her way over, but she was waylaid by one of the servers. Serena had quickly turned away and looked out the window she sat beside. When she turned back a moment later, to her disappointment, Chayse was gone.

It wasn't until the following Sunday that Serena came up with a possible way to connect with Chayse and asked about sending one of Chayse's sweet potato pies to her grandmother. She had hoped, but not really expected, that Chayse would personally come out to speak with her, so it was quite a surprise when she spotted Chayse walking toward her table. Serena quickly looked away and took a large gulp of her mimosa to steady her nerves.

"Ms. Frazier, I'm Chayse Carmichael," she had said and offered her hand in greeting.

Serena had stood, accepting her handshake, trying her best to ignore the fluttering brought on by Chayse's smooth, husky voice. "It's a pleasure to meet you, Chef Carmichael."

Chayse's grip had been strong but gentle. A feeling of warmth had spread from their clasped hands, up Serena's arm, and throughout her body. It was the strangest sensation she'd ever felt, and it took her a moment to realize Chayse had been speaking to her. She had quickly released Chayse's hand and managed to catch enough of what she said to pick up the conversation. They had discussed the pie, Serena's recent move to New York, and her grandmother. The conversation was brief and ended too soon with Serena giving Chayse her grandmother's address and phone number to send the pie.

With a good-bye and a disarming smile that made Serena's heart stutter, Chayse was walking away before Serena realized she had blown her opportunity to get Chayse's number in return. She'd sat down with a frustrated sigh. Serena was not a shy woman. She'd spent so many years hiding who she really was that when she came out she promised herself that she would no longer shy away from going after what she wanted. Since then, she'd never had a problem asking other women out, but there was something about Chayse that had her wanting to be pursued instead of doing the pursuing.

Serena knew from a recent *New York Magazine* article about Chayse and the restaurant that, in spite of having been spotted out with a WNBA player and a fashion model over the past year, there was no one special in her life right now.

The restaurant was her life, and she just didn't have the time or attention to pursue a serious relationship. Serena had to remind herself that her own life was still getting settled and that adding a romance to the mix, casual or otherwise, would just be a distraction. Even though she'd caught Chayse glancing her way on several occasions, Serena decided that, for once, she would wait for the other woman to approach her.

At least that was what she was telling herself during her early morning run. Running always helped to clear her mind, which was why she decided to go for one on Sunday, which was usually her rest day. She'd woken up from a very vivid dream about Chayse Carmichael that reminded her of her lack of physical companionship since she and Mel had split up. Going back to sleep proved difficult so in spite of it being just past dawn, she was out running through Riverside Park trying to get X-rated thoughts of a woman she barely knew out of her head.

A sudden twinge in her hamstring made her slow her pace. As she limped over to a bench to stretch the cramp out, she was grabbed from behind and pushed into a copse of bushes nearby, then thrown to the ground. The impact knocked the wind out of her, and before she could even gather her breath to cry out for help, she felt a weight on her legs and someone tugging down the waistband of her pants.

The self-defense training her police officer father had given her, kicked in. She lay still, letting her attacker think she was unconscious, and as he began to slide her pants down, she felt him shift enough to give her some leverage to turn just enough to elbow him in the jaw. Catching him off guard, she was able to scramble a few feet away and scream as loud as she could, praying there were other runners out just as early as she was. Unfortunately, her pants were bunched mid-thigh, and her attacker was able to catch her before she could make it back out to the jogging path.

He yanked her back and backhanded her across her face causing her head to whip back and slam against the ground. As Serena's vision flickered in and out, there was a shout and the sounds of a scuffle nearby, then the concerned face of a woman appeared in her line of vision asking if she was all right. Before Serena could answer, everything went dark.

As soon as Chayse saw the news story about Serena she called the crime stopper number they had displayed on the screen and told them Serena's name and gave them her grandmother's contact information which she still had from sending the pie. She then called the hospital and gave them the same information just in case there was a delay in the police getting it to them.

When they asked who she was Chayse had told them she was an acquaintance then hung up. After all, she couldn't very well tell them that Serena had been a customer she had wanted to ask out on a date. She had done the right thing by calling, and all she could do now was hope Serena recovered soon.

At least that's what Chayse told herself, but the following day she found she just couldn't get Serena off of her mind. She worried whether Serena's family had been notified and had to stop herself from calling Serena's grandmother just to make sure. Instead, she found herself standing outside Harlem Hospital Center holding a bouquet of roses but hesitant to actually go into the building.

"Sometimes that first step is always the hardest to take."

Chayse had been so lost in her thoughts that she hadn't seen the woman who had just spoken sitting on a bench a few feet from her.

"Excuse me?" Chayse said as her gaze met the other woman's. She had a short, completely white afro and wore large gold hoop earrings, a black velour hooded top with matching pants, and gold ballet flats.

The woman grinned. "You've been standing there for about five minutes so I thought you might need some encouragement to head on in."

Chayse looked away in embarrassment. "That obvious, huh?"

"She must be pretty special," the woman said as she stood and walked toward Chayse.

Chayse looked confused.

The woman gestured toward the flowers Chayse held. "Orange roses mean you're fascinated by or desire someone."

Chayse had chosen the flowers because the color reminded her of the top Serena had worn the last time she had come to the restaurant.

"If you want some private time to see my granddaughter, you'd better come along. Once her brothers get here no one will be getting within ten feet of that room without an interrogation," the older woman said as she hooked her arm through Chayse's and gently pulled her along.

"Wait, your granddaughter?" Chayse said in confusion as she allowed the woman to continue leading her toward the visitors' desk.

She ignored Chayse and spoke to the woman sitting behind the desk. "May I get a visitor's pass for Miss Carmichael here? She's visiting Serena Frazier."

"Mrs. Warren?" Chayse said in surprise.

"That's me, and you can call me Selah," Serena's grandmother answered.

Chayse laughed. "How did you know who I was?"

"I googled you after tasting your pie. Serena talked up your cooking skills so much I had to check out my competition."

"I'm glad you're here because I wanted to thank you. We wouldn't be here if it weren't for you calling the police and hospital to let them know who Serena was."

Chayse paused midstride as they walked toward the elevators, once again surprised by what Selah knew. "How did you know that was me? Are you psychic?" Chayse asked in jest.

"Hardly. My husband, God rest his soul, was a police officer, and I picked up quite a bit from him on deductive reasoning. When the hospital called me instead of Serena's parents I knew the only person here that had my contact information was you. Her cousin and roommate, Alex, is from her daddy's side of the family so she would've called him if she'd known what happened. I take it you don't know Alex."

"No. I only know Serena from the restaurant. When I saw the news story about her being attacked and they couldn't identify her, I assumed she was here without family," Chayse explained.

"Alex travels a lot for work. She's in Europe for a month so she didn't know what happened until Serena's daddy called her. We're all very grateful to you," Selah said.

"It's the least I could've done," Chayse said.

Selah patted Chayse's arm affectionately, and they continued their journey to Serena's floor in companionable silence. As they reached the room, Chayse hesitated outside the door.

"Has she woken up?" she asked.

"Not yet, but I have a feeling she will soon," Selah said confidently. "Fortunately, the doctor says her CAT scan was clear so there's no serious head trauma from the concussion she suffered."

Chayse took a deep breath and slowly released it to relax herself, then pushed the door open. The room was softly lit by a light above Serena's hospital bed. The only sounds were the soft hum and beep of the machines monitoring her vitals. Chayse slowly walked toward the bed, her heart hammering in her chest. She gazed down at Serena who looked beautifully peaceful in her slumber. As if she would wake up any moment with a stretch and a sleepy smile in greeting. Her thick hair lay in a reddish brown halo framing her face. She looked small and fragile lying tucked in and hooked up to an IV and monitor. When Chayse noticed a fading bruise along the left side of Serena's face, she felt an overwhelming need to unhook her from everything, carry her out of the hospital, and bring her back to her place to keep her sheltered and protected from any further harm. The need hit her with such ferocity she had to take a step back to keep from actually doing it.

The door to the room opened, startling Chayse so much she dropped the bouquet of flowers she had forgotten she was holding.

"Oh, I'm sorry, I didn't realize anyone was visiting right now," said a nurse just as startled to see Chayse standing there. "I just need to change her IV bag. I'll only be a moment."

Chayse knelt to pick up the flowers and place them on the bedside table. "No problem."

"She's lying there so peacefully. Reminds me of Sleeping Beauty," the nurse said.

"You seem to be missing a Prince Charming to awaken her with a kiss."

"Who says it has to be a prince?" the nurse winked as she walked past Chayse and picked up the flowers. "I'll put these in some water. Why don't you have a seat and talk to her? Having loved ones talk to unconscious patients sometimes stimulates their brain and triggers awareness, which can lead to a quicker recovery."

Chayse watched the nurse leave with the flowers and wondered if she also knew the meaning of orange roses like Serena's grandmother. The fact that her grandmother didn't seem to have an issue with another woman bringing her such flowers more than likely meant that Serena was gay, something Chayse hadn't been sure of from the few occasions they spoke. She almost laughed out loud at the irony of finding out that piece of information now.

"I guess this wouldn't be a good time to ask you out," she said her. "That'll look real good on a police report. 'Lonely lesbian trolling hospitals for dates with unwitting coma patients,'" she said with a chuckle.

Chayse sat in a chair near the bed, gazing down at Serena's peaceful visage with no idea what to say. She wasn't a loved one so Serena might not even recognize her voice.

"So...um...I just wanted to come by and see how you were. Some of the staff at the restaurant wanted me to give you their best, and they wish you a quick recovery." She hesitated before continuing. "I met your grandmother and she's as feisty as you described her." She smiled. "I think she and my grandmother would get along great. Maybe, once you're out of the hospital and if your grandmother's still in town, we can introduce them."

Chayse watched Serena's face intently, looking for any sign of awareness, then had to chuckle at herself. "I'm sitting here watching you like the sound of my voice is some miracle cure that will awaken you at any moment."

She allowed herself one last gaze, then stood to leave. "Get well soon, Serena. There's a sweet potato pie with your name on it waiting when you do."

Chayse smoothed a wayward curl away from Serena's left cheek then left the room.

❖

Serena wandered through a fog so thick she could barely see her hand in front of her face. The last thing she remembered was doing her morning run through the Riverside Park then nothing until the sound of a husky voice and the touch of a soft stroke along her cheek had drawn her here...wherever here was. She stopped and listened for the sound of the voice again, but there was nothing but silence. A sudden weariness came over her, and the fog morphed into a darkness that drew her into its inky blackness where she fell back into the nothingness she had been in before the voice called out to her.

❖

Chayse found herself back at the hospital the next day just as visiting hours began. She knew Serena's family was in town, and she didn't want to interfere with their time with her.

"Nice to see you back," said the same nurse she spoke with the other day.

"Thanks. How's she doing?" Chayse asked.

"The same. Her family's been taking shifts sitting with her. Her grandmother said she would be covering the first shift and should be here in about an hour, so you have her all to yourself until then," the nurse said.

Chayse realized the nurse might be under the misperception that she was Serena's girlfriend, and although she could have easily corrected her, Chayse found she didn't want to. She liked the idea of being Serena's Prince Charming. She walked into the room to find cards hanging on the wall and balloons and flowers on almost every surface, including her roses that seemed to be missing a few stems but the ones that were left were still holding up nicely. She laid the new bouquet she had brought with her alongside the vase, then sat in the chair near the bed. She noticed someone had combed Serena's wild hair, clasping it loosely at the nape of her neck with a hair clip.

"Judging from all the flowers, cards, and gifts, you're a pretty popular lady, Serena, which doesn't surprise me." Chayse smiled. "I can't seem to keep myself away. For the first time in a long time I didn't rush down to the restaurant because all I could think about was coming here to see how you're doing."

Chayse's brow furrowed. "I don't understand how I could barely know you, yet from the moment I saw you in the restaurant I haven't stopped thinking about you."

Chayse leaned forward and placed her forearms along the side rail of the bed and rested her chin on them. "That sounds so stalkerish."

She sat silently watching Serena for a moment. "So I guess this would be the perfect opportunity for me to tell you something about myself without worrying whether or not I'm boring you since you're already asleep," she said.

Chayse talked about her childhood, the strong influence her grandmother had in her life, and her love of cooking, promising Serena that once she got out of the hospital she would be her personal chef for a night as a welcome home gift. Chayse paused for a moment, watching Serena's face, wondering if she had really seen what she thought she saw, the faint twitch of Serena's eyelids. It was simply a muscle spasm. She looked at her watch and quickly stood. She hadn't realized how long she had been there. She didn't want to interfere with Serena's time with her family.

"Sleep well, beauty. I'll be back to see you soon." Chayse took one last look at Serena then left the room.

❖

Serena awoke within the fog once again, feeling a comforting warmth surrounding her as the mysterious voice drifted in from the outer reaches of the dense fog. Although she could hear someone speaking, she couldn't hear what exactly was being said, but it didn't matter. All that mattered was the comfort she felt at the sound of it. The fog dissipated the longer the voice spoke, and Serena found that all she wanted to do was find the person it belonged to and curl up in the safety of their arms. There was no sense of time where she was, only the voice, and when she no longer heard it, the darkness came upon her once again. Before she allowed it to completely take her, she vowed the next time she heard the voice she would find it. She didn't know how, but she knew that it would lead her out of the darkness and fog of confusion she seemed to be trapped in.

❖

Chayse sat across the table from Ebony and Belinda in Ebony's apartment hoping her friends could help her make sense of the intense pull she felt toward Serena.

"It's like I can't stay away. I've been at the hospital almost every morning this past week and when I'm not I feel like I need to be," Chayse said in frustration.

"And you just sit there and talk to her?" Ebony asked.

"Yeah, her doctor says it's good for her to hear familiar voices so I just talk about what's going on at the restaurant, what's happening in the news, and even read to her."

"There's been no response?" Belinda asked.

Chayse shrugged. "Sometimes I notice a twitch of her eyelids while I talk to her, but I figured that's just muscle spasms. That was until yesterday when one of her nurses told me they've noticed more brain activity in her scans since I've been visiting. I think she's just saying that to be nice because her family is there just as much as I am so it's more than likely their doing."

"Have they wondered about the mystery woman that keeps visiting?" Ebony asked.

Chayse chuckled. "I actually met them. Serena's grandmother brought them to the restaurant. They wanted to thank me for notifying the police about her identity. Up until then her grandmother was the only one I had been speaking to because she usually arrived when I was leaving the hospital."

"And she's cool with it?" Ebony asked.

Chayse shrugged. "She actually encourages it." Chayse went on to tell Ebony and Belinda about how she and Selah, who now insisted Chayse call her Nan, first met.

"Interesting. It seems to me that Grandma is trying to play matchmaker."

Chayse laughed out loud. "I don't think so."

"Why not? You're perfect grandma matchmaking material, a good-looking, successful, eligible woman who can cook her ass off. Any woman would be happy to have you," Belinda said.

Ebony's eyes narrowed on Belinda. "Any woman?"

Belinda leaned in toward Ebony. "You know you're the only woman for me." She placed a lingering kiss upon Ebony's lips.

"Ugh, c'mon, guys, we just ate," Chayse said in mock disgust.

"You're just jealous."

"I am." Chayse sighed wistfully. "This last year I've found myself wanting something like you two have and, ironically, when I finally find the woman of my dreams, she's in a coma."

Serena lay in a field of wildflowers letting the sun's warmth envelop her in its comforting embrace. Not too long ago, she had followed the sound of the mysterious voice to this wondrous place and basked in its beauty waiting for a sign to when she would awaken from this dream. A few moments ago, she noticed a rose bush springing up amongst the wildflowers and had gone to investigate.

On the vine grew dozens of fully bloomed orange roses. She plucked one, and another immediately grew in its place. She'd tucked the rose behind her ear and gone back to her bed of wildflowers listening to the soothing tone of the mystery voice that seemed to keep her from drowning in the darkness that arrived whenever the voice went away.

Chayse was telling Serena about Nan bringing her family to the restaurant when the door opened and in walked a visitor Chayse didn't recognize. She was a petite, shapely woman with straight black hair and a dark chocolate complexion who wore a curve-hugging, cream business suit, three-inch brown suede pumps, chocolate diamond earrings and necklace, and was carrying a designer bag and pulling a matching suitcase. Whoever this woman was, Chayse could practically see "High Maintenance" blinking like a neon sign above her head. If she was a part of Serena's family, she was nothing like the down-to-earth Frazier clan Chayse met the other night.

"Hi, can I help you?" Chayse asked.

The woman looked warily from Chayse to Serena then back again. "Who are you?"

Chayse didn't appreciate the snotty tone the woman addressed her with. "I'm a friend, and you are…"

"A *friend*?" The woman frowned as her eyes locked on Chayse's fingers entwined with Serena's.

Chayse followed her gaze, having forgotten that she held Serena's hand. She shifted to release her grip then changed her mind. Something about this woman had her wanting to stake her claim on Serena like some Neanderthal saying "This woman mine!" By this time, the woman had deposited her bags in the corner and was standing on the other side of Serena's bed with a heated narrow gaze locked on Chayse's.

❖

Serena felt a cool breeze, and the sky above her peaceful field began to darken with thick, rolling storm clouds. Something was wrong. Although she felt the presence of her mystery person, she no longer heard the sound of their voice. She sat up, feeling the need to comfort the person but didn't know how. Her hand tingled as if it was being held so she closed her fingers around the invisible grasp in comfort.

❖

Chayse noticed the other woman's possessive gaze, and a niggling of doubt entered her mind. She knew nothing about Serena. What if she was already in a relationship and all of this was for nothing? She was just about to release Serena's hand when Serena's fingers suddenly folded around Chayse's.

Chayse tore her eyes from the visitor's to Serena's peaceful expression. "Serena?"

Although there was no other physical response, Serena still held Chayse's hand in a tender clasp, as if she knew Chayse needed comfort. Chayse smiled down at her.

"Look, I don't know who you are, but I'd like you to leave so that I may visit *MY* friend."

For a moment, Chayse had forgotten the other woman was there. "Look, I don't know who you are, but—"

She was interrupted by the arrival of Selah Warren. The jovial smile she gave Chayse turned to a frown at the sight of the other woman in the room.

"Melanie, what in the world are you doing here?" Nan asked, obviously annoyed.

"Hello, Mrs. Warren. As soon as I heard what happened I flew out here to be with Serena."

"Mm-hm," Nan said doubtfully as she walked over to where Chayse was. "How you doing, honey?" she asked, placing an affection kiss on Chayse's cheek.

"I'm good, Nan. How about you?" Chayse answered, hugging her.

"I'd be better with some good news about our sweet girl here," Nan said wistfully.

"Well, it may be just a muscle spasm or unconscious reaction, but she gripped my hand back." Chayse brought Nan's attention to her and Serena's entwined fingers.

Nan's face lit up. "I knew you would be the one to bring her back."

"Let's not turn me into a miracle worker yet."

Nan patted their joined hands. "It's only a matter of time."

Nan shifted her attention to Melanie who she had been ignoring since she walked into the room. "Now, Miss Melanie, it was my understanding that you and Serena ended your relationship before she left Georgia because you didn't agree with her coming to New York, so I'm a bit confused as to why you're here."

Chayse gently eased her hand from Serena's as she prepared to leave. "Nan, I should probably head out."

"Honey, you stay right there. You have just as much right to be here as anyone else."

Melanie sighed in frustration. "Mrs. Warren, it was Serena who decided to break it off. I still care about her very much."

Chayse didn't miss the side glance Melanie gave her at her declaration of feelings for Serena.

"Nan, I really do have to go. We're delivering lunches to the homeless shelter today, and I need to get back to the restaurant to help prepare the food," Chayse said.

"All right. We'll still see you on Saturday?"

Chayse smiled. "Bright and early."

"Good. I'll walk you out," Nan said.

Chayse nodded and took one last look at Serena. In what had become a habit, she grasped Serena's hand, leaned down, whispered in her ear, "Wake up, Sleeping Beauty," and then placed a soft kiss on her temple, ignoring Melanie's angry glare.

"I didn't catch your name," Melanie said to Chayse as she was following Nan toward the door.

"If you had asked nicely I might have given it," she said before walking out of the room.

Serena sat watching as the clouds dissipated and the sun shone once again over her little field of paradise. The sweet smell of the lone rose bush amongst the wildflowers and the warmth of the sunshine made her drowsy. As she lay down to rest, she noticed the strangest thing happening in the palm of her left hand, the very hand she had felt the tender grip of someone's touch just moments ago. It began to tingle, and a beautiful rose tattoo wove its way into the delicate skin of her palm. Once the tattoo was complete, she held her hand over her heart and felt such tenderness it brought a tear to her eye. Just before she drifted off to sleep, she heard the voice that had become her lifeline in this strange world of unconsciousness whisper, as clear as if the person stood right beside her. "Wake up, Sleeping Beauty."

Later that evening, Chayse sat in her office wondering about her fascination with Serena. How could she possibly have such intense feelings for a woman she had only spoken with a few times? Well, at least while she was conscious.

Trying to fight the pull Serena seemed to have on her was liking denying herself air to breathe. Her priorities had changed since she began to visit Serena almost daily. One change in particular caught Chayse completely off guard. She had reached her goal with the success of her restaurant and was exactly where she wanted to be in her life, yet since Serena entered her world Chayse found herself wishing she had someone to share her success with, to come home to, to be able to wake up on a Sunday morning and prepare breakfast in bed for two rather than brunch for two hundred, or to simply share a conversation about how their day went. A knock on her office door interrupted her thoughts.

"Come in," she said.

It was her hostess, Raquel "Hey, boss lady, are you going to hide in here all night? Customers are asking about you."

"I'm not feeling too sociable. I think I'm gonna take off for the night," Chayse said.

"Is there anything I can do for you?" Raquel asked in concern.

"No, I think I'm just burned out and need a break. I'll be fine by tomorrow," she said reassuringly.

"All right. Call me if you need anything," Raquel said before leaving the office.

Chayse stopped in the kitchen to check on her staff, then headed out through the back entrance of the restaurant to avoid running into anyone. She didn't feel like sitting in her apartment moping so decided to go for a walk. Before she knew it, she was standing outside the hospital debating whether to go up or not. Visiting hours were almost over, and she was sure Serena's family was probably still with her. She turned to leave.

"Chayse? Is that you?"

She turned back to find Serena's mother heading toward her. "Hi, Mrs. Frazier."

"What are you doing here so late?" Colleen Frazier asked as she gave Chayse a warm hug in greeting.

"I was out for a walk and ended up here," Chayse answered.

Colleen smiled knowingly. "You really care about my daughter."

"I guess more than I anticipated."

"Why don't we chat," Colleen suggested.

Chayse nodded, following her to the same bench where she had first met Serena's grandmother. She had spent some time with Serena's family when they came by the restaurant to meet her, but other than Nan she had never spent any one-on-one time with any of them. Their next gathering was planned for that Saturday morning at the restaurant when she and Nan were going to make breakfast for everyone.

"Being our firstborn and only girl, Serena and I were very close while she was growing up," Colleen said. "Then, her last year of high school, she told me about a crush she had on one of her female friends and I didn't handle it very well. I told her it was nothing, just a phase, and that she just hadn't met the right boy yet. I could see I'd hurt her saying that, but I didn't know what else to say." Her voice was filled with regret.

Chayse winced. She had heard that same response so many times from well-meaning family and friends when she came out, she completely understood how Serena must have felt hearing her mother say it.

Colleen's smile was sad. "From your reaction I guess you've heard that one before."

"Yes, and still do once in a while," Chayse said.

Colleen nodded in understanding. "Our relationship wasn't the same for a long time after that. It only got worse when she came out after her college graduation. I refused to believe my little girl was gay because that meant we would never share all the mother-daughter life experiences that most mothers look forward to, like planning her wedding and guiding her through her first pregnancy and motherhood. Instead of giving her the love and understanding she needed and deserved, I'd pushed Serena away for purely selfish reasons.

"After she told us, she and I barely spoke to each other for over a year. She even moved out to live with her grandmother to be able to live openly without having to see the disappointment in my eyes whenever she went on a date or brought a friend home. Regrettably, it took Serena getting sick for me to realize how stupid and selfish I was being." Unshed tears shimmered in Colleen's eyes, and Chayse instinctively reached for her hand in comfort. Colleen gave Chayse's hand a gentle squeeze in appreciation.

"She went to see her doctor about abdominal bloating and pain and, after several tests, was diagnosed with invasive epithelial ovarian cancer. She was already in Stage 2 when they caught it, but it was treatable. Unfortunately, the treatment required her having a hysterectomy as well as months of chemotherapy. Although she refused my request to move back home so that I could take care of her, I was still with her every day and by her side for every chemo treatment. To see her go through what she went through without a complaint or show of fear made me so proud. My daughter is a strong, beautiful person, and most of all, a fighter. She lives life with so much joy and love, and I wouldn't have her be any other way," Colleen said, a sense of pride in her voice.

"Whoever she decides to settle down with will be blessed to have her and all the love she has to give, and if she deems them worthy of that love, then I'll accept them as well as long as they prove their worth by loving my daughter just as deeply as she will love them," she added, meeting Chayse's gaze with open honesty.

"Your daughter is a very blessed woman to have you for a mother," Chayse said.

"No, I'm the blessed one, Chayse. Now," Colleen said, releasing Chayse's hand with another quick squeeze. "My ride is here and you should get up there before visiting hours are over."

They stood together and embraced once more before Colleen walked over to a waiting car.

"Hey, Chayse!" Serena's father cheerfully greeted from the car.

"Hey, Mr. Frazier!" Chayse waved once more to the two before the car pulled away from the curb.

Chayse made it up to Serena's room with twenty minutes left before visiting hours were over. She planned to stay just a few minutes, long enough to look in on Serena and say good night. She walked into the room and was about to take her usual position next to the bed when she noticed a few changes.

"Your mom's been busy," she said as she ran a finger along a soft curl in Serena's hair.

Chayse grasped Serena's hand, placing a soft kiss on her knuckles above the splash of deep plum color on her nails that matched the soft pink floral nightgown she now wore.

Chayse smiled. "Now you really do look like Sleeping Beauty," she said as she bent to place her lips near Serena's ear…

When Serena felt the warmth of the bright sunlight spilling over her and was enveloped by the strong scent of her rosebush carried on the breeze, she knew it was time. She closed her eyes, lifted her face toward the sunshine, and listened, patiently waiting for the voice that would carry her from her little field…

"Wake up, Sleeping Beauty," Chayse whispered. "There's so much I'd rather say to you while you're awake."

Chayse placed a soft kiss along Serena's cheek, inhaling the fresh clean scent of the soap Colleen must have used on her. She shifted so that she could see Serena's face.

"Please wake up, Serena." Chayse placed her lips on Serena's in a gentle kiss.

The tender moment turned to shock as Chayse felt Serena's hand flex within her own at the same time as Serena's lips opened and a subtle moan escaped. Chayse eased away from Serena just as her eyes slowly began to flutter open.

"Serena?" Chayse said hesitantly as Serena's gaze began to focus on her.

Since her right hand was still within Serena's soft grasp, Chayse subtly pushed the call button with her left so as not to make any sudden movement that would make Serena finally waking up seem like a dream. The nurse was there immediately.

"I see someone has finally decided to wake up," she walked over to the bed and gazed down at Serena.

Serena looked from Chayse to the nurse then back to Chayse and began to speak but winced in pain instead.

"Don't try to talk. Your voice hasn't been used in a while. Let her sip some water." The nurse handed Chayse a cup with a straw. "I'll get the doctor." She smiled reassuringly.

Serena sipped the water Chayse offered. As her gaze became clear and focused she looked around the room then settled her eyes on Chayse. Since Chayse was the only person in the room when she woke up, Serena knew that she had to be the one who had been talking to her all this time. She tried clearing her throat and talking again, but the only thing that came out was a croak.

"The nurse said you shouldn't talk," Chayse gently reprimanded her.

Serena needed to know for sure if Chayse had been the one to pull her from her sleep. She pointed to Chayse, made the talking gesture with her hands, pointed to herself, and made the gesture for sleeping hoping Chayse would understand what she was trying to say.

Chayse smiled sheepishly. "Uh, yes, I was talking to you while you were sleeping. The doctor said it would be good for you."

Smiling, Serena pointed to Chayse, her lips, and then to herself.

Chayse blushed and looked away. "Yes, I kissed you," she said.

Serena grasped Chayse's hand, interlocking their fingers. Chayse turned her gaze back to Serena's and was met with such tenderness, her heart swelled in response. The moment was interrupted by the arrival of the nurse with a doctor.

"Well, Ms. Frazier, welcome back. I'm Dr. Garrett and I'm going to take care of you until we reach Dr. Jansen," the doctor said.

"I better go and let the doctor do his thing," Chayse said to Serena with a shy smile.

Serena grasped her hand tighter as Chayse started to pull away.

"I'm just going to step out in the hall and call your parents. They'll want to know you're awake," Chayse said.

Serena nodded and released her hand, but her eyes followed Chayse until she left the room.

Chayse leaned against the wall outside Serena's room trying to calm her racing heart. Did Serena wake up because of her? No, it was just a coincidence. Her family had also been here for days talking to her, and it was obvious all the stimulation must have helped.

"I just happened to be at the right place at the right time," Chayse said to herself, dismissing the silly notion that she really had awakened her very own Sleeping Beauty. She looked once more over at the room, then took out her phone to call Serena's grandmother knowing she would inform the rest of her family of her condition.

The nurse came out just as she ended her call. "You may go in now but only for a few more moments."

Chayse nodded and followed her back into the room. Serena was now sitting propped up in the bed looking beautiful and refreshed, as if she had just woken up from a short nap rather than a comatose sleep. She smiled shyly at Chayse as the doctor finished his exam.

"We'll schedule a few tests in the morning just to make sure everything is fine," he was telling Serena as Chayse took her usual place at her bedside. "Until then, and I know it sounds strange to say under the circumstance, but get some rest," he said. With a quick nod at Chayse, he and the nurse left the room.

Chayse didn't know what to say to Serena now that she was awake. Serena surprised her by speaking first.

"The nurse told me what happened," she said quietly, her voice still a bit raspy from being unused for so long. "I don't remember anything after I got hit by my attacker."

"Fortunately, he was caught by some Good Samaritans that were nearby when they heard you scream. How are you feeling?" Chayse asked.

"Like I overslept way too long," Serena said with a grin.

Chayse chuckled. "Yeah, just a bit."

Serena held her hand out to Chayse who clasped it. "Thank you," she said. "The nurse also told me what you did for me. Identifying me, contacting my family, I don't think I can thank you enough for that." Tears sparkled in her eyes.

Chayse's heart ached with tenderness for her. "When I saw the news story I just wanted to help."

"But you've done so much more. She said you've been here every day since then; bringing me these beautiful flowers, talking to me." She wiped a fallen tear from her cheek.

"I didn't do anything different from what your family has been doing. Your grandmother, your parents, your brothers, and your cousin have all been here visiting and talking to you. The doctor thought it would stimulate you into waking up. Guess he was right," Chayse said.

"But there was only one voice I heard while I was unconscious. Only one voice was able to reach me through the darkness," Serena said.

"Probably Nan's. There were quite a few times she tried fussing at you to wake up," Chayse said with a chuckle.

Grasping Chayse's hand with both of hers, Serena smiled. "I believe it, but it wasn't hers, it was yours. When I woke up to find you here, I knew it was your voice that held the darkness at bay. Chayse, it was your voice, your kiss that brought me back."

Before Chayse could respond, the nurse popped her head in. "I'm sorry, but the doctor wants her to rest." Then she left them alone once again.

Chayse nodded and gazed back down at Serena. "I'll be back in the morning."

"Only if you bring a slice of sweet potato pie with you," Serena said with a grin.

Chayse laughed. "With your family here I'll have to bring two whole pies to share."

"Good night, Serena," Chayse said.

"Aren't you forgetting something?" Serena said.

Chayse's brow furrowed in confusion.

"Just because Sleeping Beauty is awake doesn't mean she still can't get a kiss," Serena said.

Chayse's eyes widened in surprise.

"I told you it was you who brought me back." Serena pulled Chayse toward her.

Chayse didn't know how or why such a thing was possible, but she wasn't going to deny it. When their lips met, it felt to Chayse as if some unseen tether sealed and bonded them together. The kiss only lasted a moment, but once they parted they were breathing as if they had run for miles.

Chayse touched her forehead to Serena's. "I better go," she said breathlessly.

"Okay," Serena said.

Chayse placed one more kiss on Serena's forehead, then slowly backed away from the bed.

"Good night, my prince," Serena said with a soft smile.

"Good night, my beauty."

❖

The next morning, Chayse was up early baking two fresh sweet potato pies to give to Serena and her family and the nurses that had been taking such great care of her. She glided around her kitchen as if she were walking on air. Lucky even noticed the difference, sitting on a stool watching her curiously as one of Chayse's favorite songs came on the radio and her gliding slid into dancing.

"Ah, you like that move?" she asked the cat as she did a quick spin.

Lucky blinked slowly then meowed in response, not the least bit impressed by her roommate's fancy dance moves.

"Hey, I used to be real smooth back in the day. Maybe I'll take Serena dancing when she's feeling up to it."

Lucky's response was another slow blink then a yawn. Chayse laughed out loud at the fact that she was actually standing there having a conversation with a cat. Serena was just what she needed to keep from becoming the crazy cat lady. She placed the pies in an insulated bag to keep warm and made her way down to the restaurant. She decided to wait until late morning to visit Serena to give her family some alone time with her. Chayse tried to keep busy, but the hours seemed to tick by so slowly that she found it difficult to concentrate on anything. By ten thirty a.m., her staff was just as ready for her to leave as she was.

"Another half hour won't make a difference. Just go," Raquel told her. "If you go around and rearrange one more place setting, Libby is going to strangle you."

Chayse looked up to find one of her servers standing just a few feet away, hands on hips, glaring at her in annoyance.

Chayse slowly set the charger plate she had in her hand back on the table and nodded to Libby in surrender.

She turned to Raquel with a grin. "Yeah, I guess I should probably get there before she gets too tired from all the tests they had to run and her family visiting."

"Good idea. We'll be fine here," Raquel reassured her.

When Chayse arrived at the hospital, she swung by the nurses' station to drop off a pie for them then practically ran to Serena's room. She was stopped short in the doorway by the sight of Serena sitting up cross-legged in her bed laughing and holding hands with her ex-girlfriend. Determined not to assume anything, she opened her mouth to speak, but her words were halted when Melanie reached up to gently smooth away a stray curl from Serena's face. It wasn't the act itself that caused the sudden ache in Chayse's heart but the look on Melanie's face. She still loved Serena, and Chayse didn't believe there was any way she could compete with the obvious love and history Serena and Melanie had. With her heart slowly breaking, Chayse began to back out of the room, but the movement must have caught Serena's attention because she turned to look her way.

"Chayse, I almost thought you weren't coming."

Serena's bright happy smile almost dispelled the insecurity Chayse was feeling, but the cocky grin on Melanie's face as she continued to sit on the bed holding Serena's hand pushed it right back to the forefront.

"Uh…yeah, I can't stay long. I just wanted to drop off the pie I promised." On shaky legs, she walked into the room and set the insulated bag on the table at the end of the bed next to Serena's breakfast tray.

"You're not staying long?" Serena moved to stand, but wobbled on her feet and fell back onto the bed.

Melanie pulled her close. "Whoa! Not so fast. You know the doctor said not to push yourself too much."

"I'm fine, I just stood up too fast," Serena said.

"I have to get back to the restaurant. We have a VIP group coming in, and there's a lot to do," Chayse said as she turned and quickly headed for the door, her heart aching as she ignored Serena calling her name and kept walking.

"Was that Chayse I saw leaving in such a hurry?" Nan asked Serena as she entered the room.

"Yes. She dropped off some pies and couldn't stay long." Serena was hurt and disappointed by Chayse's sudden departure.

Melanie gently squeezed her hand. "Maybe it's for the best. You should probably only have close friends and family visiting anyway, at least until you're back on your feet."

"If it weren't for Chayse, Serena's family wouldn't have even known she was here, so she has more right to be here than you do," Nan said, not bothering to hide her dislike for Melanie.

Melanie's cockiness wavered a bit under Nan's glare so she focused her attention back on Serena. "I'm going to head back to the hotel so you can get some rest. I'll come back this evening."

"I appreciate you flying up here to check on me, but you really don't need to stay. I'm fine. You should head back home," Serena told her, slowly realizing Melanie's presence might have been the reason Chayse left the way she did.

"I'm here because I want to be, not because I need to be. I care about you, Serena," Melanie said, reaching up to caress Serena's face.

Serena blocked Melanie's hand. "Mel, I wasn't hit on the head so hard that I forgot why we broke up. This doesn't change anything."

"But I've changed," Melanie said. "I realize how selfish I was being, and I'm willing to try to make it work."

"Make what work? I've also changed. I've had time to think about and discover who I am, and I love the me that I've become since moving to New York. I don't plan to move back to Georgia or be with a woman who doesn't support my dreams."

"You plan on staying here? Is it Chayse? You barely know her. From what I understand you barely spoke to her before you ended up in the hospital. For all you know she could be some sick stalker who gets off on vulnerable women. You've always been so naïve," Melanie said angrily.

Serena sighed. "I think you should go."

"Serena, I'm sorry. Why don't I come back in the morning and we can talk after you've rested," Melanie said hopefully.

"There's nothing to talk about. Thank you again for coming to see me. Have a safe trip home."

Mel slowly stood. "Serena."

Serena turned a determined and steady gaze towards Melanie but didn't respond.

Mel turned to leave. "Bye, Serena," she said, her voice breaking.

"Bye, Mel." Serena watched her walk out the door and closed her eyes with a heavy sigh. "Nan, why do relationships have to be so contrary?"

Nan chuckled as she sat beside Serena on the bed. "I wish I had an easy answer for that. All I know is that when it's right, when you find a person who makes all the contrariness worth it, you can't let them slip through your fingers because you might not have that chance again."

Serena slowly opened her eyes. "You're talking about Chayse, aren't you?"

"You tell me."

Serena shook her head. "Like Mel said, I barely know her. How's it possible to fall in love with someone I barely know?"

"Who said anything about love?" Nan said with a raised brow.

Serena looked down at her lap. "She led me through the darkness, Nan. I was told you all spent time talking to me while I was unconscious, but Chayse's voice was the only one that came through."

"And what does that tell you?"

Serena wasn't sure she wanted to believe what she was thinking. "Maybe I'm so used to all of your voices that a different voice was able to penetrate because it was something unfamiliar."

"That sounds like a good explanation, but do you really believe that?" Nan asked.

Serena met Nan's questioning gaze. "Nan, this isn't some fairy tale with a sleeping princess who can be awakened with a kiss. This is real life. Stuff like that doesn't happen," she said, knowing that's pretty much what actually happened.

"She kissed you?" Nan asked with a grin.

Serena blushed. "It was just a quick peck at the same moment I was waking up."

"Uh-huh," Nan said. "I take it that wasn't the last kiss that happened."

"Nan, I don't know what to think about all of this," she said in frustration.

"See, there's your problem. Stop thinking so much and do what you did when you decided to move here. Go with what you're feeling."

From that first moment Serena saw Chayse on the other side of the restaurant, she had felt an immediate pull toward her, and as far-fetched as it seemed, she couldn't deny that it was definitely that same pull toward Chayse that brought her out of her deep sleep. There was also something Serena saw in Chayse's eyes when she did fully awaken. She couldn't say it was love, but there was something between them that had Chayse under its spell as well.

"You saw how she walked out of here. What if it's too late?" Serena asked.

Nan smiled knowingly. "You don't have to worry about that. Let's get you a clean bill of health and out of here, then we'll work on getting Sleeping Beauty her princess."

❖

Chayse slowly made her way up the stairs to her apartment above the restaurant having just returned from catering a celebrity charity event uptown. All she wanted to do now was throw on some sweats, make a cup of chai tea, curl up on the sofa with Lucky, and watch late night movies until she fell asleep and started everything over again in the morning. When she opened the door, she immediately knew something was off. Lucky wasn't at the door for her usual greeting, and she picked up the lightest scent of vanilla and coconut as she walked through the door. She perused the open space of her loft, stopping in surprise when she reached her living room space. The sight before her had her wondering if she had finally gone nuts and her imagination had manifested some fantasy she had or if she was really seeing Serena lying asleep on her sofa with Lucky curled up in her lap. She stared for another full minute before she quietly closed the door and walked toward the sleeping figures. Sensing her presence, Lucky sat up, slowly blinked at her as if to say "What? You weren't here so somebody had to keep her company," and then casually jumped from the sofa and went to her cat condo in the corner of the room.

Chayse gazed back at Serena, still in disbelief that she was actually in her apartment. It had been almost two weeks since she had visited Serena in the hospital and found her and her ex-girlfriend getting reacquainted. The next day, Nan left a message for Chayse that Serena would be going home that afternoon. Chayse responded back with a text thanking her for letting her know and to *Give Serena my best wishes.*

Feisty as ever, Nan had texted back, *Why don't you give them to her in person* with Serena's home address. Chayse didn't answer the text and felt guilty about it ever since. She had spent every day since doing anything she could to keep busy and not to think about Serena, which failed miserably. She constantly found herself thinking things like, did she and Mel work things out? If so, would that mean she would go back to Georgia? Did she think about Chayse as much as Chayse thought about her, which was pretty much every waking hour of the day? And now, as if all that thinking about Serena had manifested itself into reality, here she was.

Chayse perused Serena's face which had filled out a bit since she had last seen her, and her expression was just as peaceful and serene as it had been before she had awoken in the hospital. Her gaze slowly made its way along Serena's prone figure. She must have come from work because she was dressed in a white silk blouse that must have come unbuttoned while she slept, allowing a generous view of her lace camisole underneath and the rise and fall of her voluptuous chest with every breath she took. She followed the curve of her narrow waist to full hips encased in a burgundy pencil skirt that had hiked up around her thighs to display smooth, shapely legs that led to her delicate feet and the wine painted toenails that matched the color on her fingernails and lipstick.

The urge to run her hand along the curves her eyes had just followed was so strong Chayse had to ball her hand into a fist to keep from doing it. She forced her gaze back up to Serena's face, surrounded by a halo of her thick curly hair. Chayse knelt in front of Serena, reached up to smooth a stray curl away, and whispered, "Wake up, Sleeping Beauty."

Serena's lips curved into a soft smile. "I didn't mean to fall asleep. What time is it?"

"It's after midnight. How did you get in here?" Chayse asked.

Serena stayed in her prone position and propped her head up on her hand. "Raquel let me in. I came by the restaurant after work to see you, but she said you were catering an event and probably wouldn't be back until late. I didn't want to leave without talking to you so I asked if I could wait in your office, and she offered to let me wait up here because you probably wouldn't go back to the restaurant until morning. I hope that wasn't too presumptuous of me."

"No, it's fine. I see you met Lucky."

"Yes. I didn't know she was even here until after Raquel left. She showed me around your beautiful apartment then left. I felt something rubbing against my leg and almost had a heart attack."

Chayse gazed curiously over at Lucky sleepily watching them from the top of her tower. "She must have sensed something pretty special in you because she usually doesn't come out for visitors."

Serena gazed over at Lucky as well. "Well then, I'm honored, Miss Lucky. Thank you."

Lucky did one of her slow blinks, meowed in response, and closed her eyes. Chayse and Serena both laughed at the feline's nonchalant attitude. When their gazes met again, it was like that first glance when Serena had awoken. That familiar pull on her heart that seemed to reach down to her very soul flared to life. Their eyes now locked, Serena reached forward, grasped Chayse by the back of head, and brought her toward her. Their lips met for a kiss so intense that the disbelief and doubt she had about what had happened between them while Serena was in the hospital faded away. She felt that this feeling, this moment right here, was all that mattered and all that would matter from this point on.

Chayse pulled away and asked, "Melanie?"

"Gone. It's only you. It's been only you since the moment I first saw you at the restaurant."

Chayse closed her eyes and took a deep breath. When she looked at Serena again, Serena's heart skipped a beat at the intensity in Chayse's eyes. The gentle, spirited light that was there moments ago was replaced by a passion that turned her pupils into a dark abyss Serena would gladly lose herself in. Without breaking eye contact, Chayse got up from her kneeling position, lifted Serena into her arms, and made her way to her bedroom. Once there she gently laid Serena on the bed and kissed her once again. Her tongue explored Serena's mouth, licking and nipping gently at her full lips. Serena lost herself completely in that kiss and had no idea when Chayse managed to undo the tiny pearl buttons of her blouse to slip her hand beneath her camisole to brush the pad of her thumb along the tops of her breast. What she did know was that she wanted more...so much more.

She moaned with need into Chayse's mouth, and it was as if Chayse understood what she was asking because her mouth began leaving a heated trail of kisses along her cheek, neck, and cleavage. Serena's nipples strained against the constraint of her bra until she felt Chayse's deft fingers reach behind her and undo the clasps in one swift motion to free them. When the heat of Chayse's mouth enveloped her right nipple, Serena almost shouted for joy. When Chayse's tongue joined the party and her long fingers gently grasped her left nipple, it was her undoing. The speed and ferocity at which her orgasm came took Serena by surprise, and she tried to fight it, but Chayse's manipulations were too much so she allowed the pleasure to take over. She had never felt anything so intense, not even with Mel. When she came to her senses, Chayse was gazing down at her.

"You are so beautiful," Chayse said in awe.

"Even while I'm awake?" she said with a smile.

"Especially when you're awake," Chayse's hand traveled from Serena's breast along her torso to beneath the hem of her skirt, which was now up around her hips, to where her panties were soaked from her orgasm, "and it seems to me that there are some other things that may need awakening," she said with a sexy grin as she slowly rubbed Serena's sex through her panties.

Serena's breath caught in a shuddering sigh of pleasure. "I have way too many clothes on."

Chuckling, Chayse shifted so that she could help Serena remove her now disheveled clothing as well as her own. "Lie back," she told Serena with a look of pure hunger in her eyes.

Chayse crouched over Serena and lowered her head toward hers for another soul-stirring kiss before proceeding to lavish loving attention to the rest of Serena's luscious body.

After what seemed like forever, Serena could take the torture no longer. "Chayse…" she pleaded.

Chayse slid her body up along Serena's, cupped her hand over Serena's sex, and whispered, "Open your legs for me."

Serena willingly obeyed, widening her legs so that Chayse could lie between them. Once she was settled, Chayse slowly slid one of her fingers in and out of Serena's heated vagina, gently flicking the pad of her thumb across her full clit and savoring another taste of Serena's pebble hard nipples, where previously she had been completing each touch individually. Serena's moans grew more frantic and louder as Chayse continued her lovemaking. When Serena's pleasure reached the highest peak and her body tensed Chayse whispered in her ear, "Wake up, Sleeping Beauty."

Those four words meant everything to Serena and sent her over the edge…awakening a passion and a love like she had never known.

STILETTO

Based on the Cinderella *fairy tale*

Cass Phillips took one look at her agenda for the week and felt another headache coming on. Dr. Jansen told her they were stress related and she needed to slow down, maybe take a vacation, something she hadn't done in over a year. Unfortunately, this was not the time for vacations. She had the Pure Music Annual Charity Ball coming up in a little over a month where she and Ebony planned to debut two new artists as well as promoting tours for three other artists hitting the road right after the charity ball. With a tired sigh, she laid her head on her desk and closed her eyes, hoping just a few moments of quiet would help alleviate the pain. Not even a minute later, there was a knock on her open office door.

"Yo, Cass, you all right?" Ebony asked as she stood in the doorway.

Cass sat up rubbing her eyes. "Yeah, just a headache. What's up?"

"I can come back later," Ebony said.

"No, have a seat. Let me just grab some aspirin." Cass opened her desk drawer, pulled out a pill bottle, swallowed two capsules with some water, and focused back on Ebony. "What's going on?"

"It's not a problem yet, but there's some tension building between Cree and Frenetic, and I don't mean the good kind," Ebony explained.

"Let me guess, Frenetic tried to push up on Cree and she turned him down," Cass said in frustration.

"Yes and no. He tried while they were in the middle of recording their set not knowing her boyfriend was in the studio and could see and hear everything going on. When they came out of the booth, the boyfriend jumped in Frenetic's face, but Cree was able to step in before it got physical. Frenetic wants him banned from the studio while they record, and Cree is second-guessing them going on tour together."

"Damn, I told Frenetic to keep it in his pants while they worked together because Cree wasn't the side chick type." Cass hit the intercom on her phone.

"What can I do for you, Cass?" her assistant answered.

"Stephanie, would you please set up a meeting with Frenetic and Cree as soon as possible? Shift whatever on my calendar needs to be shifted to make this happen. Include Ebony in that meeting as well."

"Will do. Don't forget you and Ebony are meeting with the event planner about the charity ball in an hour at Chayse's Place."

Cass ran her hand across her close-cropped head. "Yeah, okay. Can you have one of the cars pull around in about twenty minutes?"

"Man, you look tired. Why don't you let me and Stephanie handle the charity ball? The event planner is doing a great job so everything is pretty much finished. All we really need to do is show up," Ebony said.

Cass knew Ebony was right, but she found it hard to let go. Cass wasn't the type of CEO who sat lounging in her penthouse office letting everyone else do all the work. She liked being involved and having a say in every aspect of Pure Music Records. The company was failing and about to go bankrupt when she took it over from the previous owner and CEO who had been too busy partying and spending more money than they could make to care what was going on with the business. She promised her employees and artists that if they stuck with her she would show them the true potential of Pure Music by personally investing her own money and time every step of the way. She kept her promise, and now Pure Music was one of the highest grossing independent labels in the industry. Knowing that it was her own personal sacrifices and the fear of failure that brought them to where they were was what was keeping her from stepping back and letting someone else takeover some of her responsibilities.

"No, I'm good." She stood and stretched the kinks out of her back. "A dose of Chayse's lobster mac 'n' cheese is just what I need right now."

❖

"Yo, Cass!"

Cass opened her eyes to find everyone staring at her. "Shit, did I fall asleep again?"

"Yeah, you did," Chayse said.

Cass shifted in her seat. "I'm sorry, y'all. I haven't been sleeping well lately," she explained with embarrassment.

"May I make a suggestion?" Eve Monroe, their event planner, asked.

Cass yawned. "Unless you have some formula for cloning myself to get more done I don't think there is anything you can suggest that I haven't tried."

"I did a promotional event for Beaches Resorts, and they gifted me with a complimentary stay at their resort in Turks and Caicos that we've been holding for the past three months. Unfortunately, between my events and Lynette's book tour we haven't been able to sync up our schedules to use the stay. Why don't you take it and get some rest before the ball?" Eve suggested.

Cass raised a hand to stop any comments Ebony was about to make. "Thanks for the offer, Eve, but I don't have time to take off for one day let alone a week."

Eve shrugged in resignation. "The offer is on the table if you change your mind. I'll get the swag bag samples over to Stephanie tomorrow for final review. After that we'll be all set," she said as she gathered her things.

Cass, Chayse, and Ebony all stood as she stood to leave.

"Thanks again, Eve. Chayse said Details by Eve was one of the best planners in town, and she was right judging by how smoothly all of this has been going compared to previous years."

"Thank you. Remember that when any of your business associates are looking for a referral," she said.

Cass watched the sway of her hips as she walked away. "Damn, that woman is fine."

"That woman is also very happily married," Chayse said.

Cass sighed wistfully as Eve disappeared from view. "I could probably change that in one night."

Ebony laughed. "Man, even if she was interested you wouldn't know what to do with all those curves. Your flavor is usually one of those tall, lanky runway models who need to have Chayse feed them a real meal once in a while."

"Yeah, if you bring another one of those wispy things in here again to order 'just a salad, please' off of my menu I'm gonna pour some bacon fat on it just to see how quickly it'll thicken her up."

Cass laughed. "Oh, y'all got jokes now that you got yourselves henpecked. I bet Belinda and Serena would love to hear how y'all used to roll with me back in the day."

"Belinda knows exactly who I was before we got together," Ebony said confidently.

"Serena knows I had no social life before she came along so don't go telling any lies on me."

Cass yawned again. "No worries. All I'm going to be doing right now is going home to bed. I'll see you in the office tomorrow, Eb."

"I know you, Cass. Don't go back to the office. Anything that needs to be done can wait until tomorrow," Ebony insisted.

Cass bid her two best friends good-bye and did exactly what Ebony told her not to do. There was no point in heading home since she wasn't going to get much sleep anyway. Instead of calling for her car service, Cass decided to take the subway downtown. Because most of her work for Pure Music happened behind the scenes, it afforded her more anonymity than Ebony or one of her other artists so she took the subway more often than not. She also knew the minute she would have sat in the car's comfortable interior she would have fallen right to sleep. She figured taking the subway during rush hour would help her stay awake. When she got down to the platform it was as packed as she expected and the train was pulling into the station. She managed to squeeze in just before the doors closed and found herself sardined between the door and an elderly woman trying to balance herself with her cane as the train jostled out of the station.

Two stations later, the train was less crowded, but there still were no seats and those sitting nearby seemed to ignore the common courtesy of offering the elderly woman a seat. Cass was just about to say something, when what she could only describe as an African goddess walked over and suggested to a teenage boy sitting nearby that he should offer the woman his seat. He simply looked back down at his phone, tapping the screen. The goddess smiled sweetly, leaned forward, popped his earphone out of his ear, and whispered. The boy's eyes widened in shock or fear, Cass couldn't tell which, and when the goddess straightened back up, he stood, walked over to the elderly passenger, and offered his seat. She took the seat and smiled up at the goddess in appreciation while the teen hurriedly went to the next car avoiding any eye contact with her.

As the train traveled along, Cass and the goddess's gaze met across the car. Cass's heart skipped a beat; she was mesmerized. The goddess stood at eye level with Cass, about six feet in height. Cass figured most of that height was from the six-inch red platform stiletto heeled boots the goddess wore. She wore her hair in a sculpted flat top that brought attention to her face, her complexion was a rich mahogany, her deep brown upturned eyes shone brightly, and her full dark berry-painted lips turned up in a sexy grin. The spell was broken when the train stopped and the goddess's visage was lost in the crowd exiting the train.

It wasn't Cass's stop, but she decided to exit as well in an attempt to catch the other woman, but by the time she made it off the train it was too late. The mystery woman seemed to have disappeared. Cass jumped back on the train just as the doors were closing and managed to grab a seat. As the train began slowly rolling out of the station, to Cass's chagrin, she caught a glimpse of the goddess's red boots through the window as she walked up the stairs from the platform.

❖

Faith Shaw was on a mission and walked with purposeful strides toward Columbus Circle. An urgent message from her attorney had her cutting short an important meeting with a prospective buyer that she had been courting for months so that she could meet him regarding her mother's estate. Her heart ached at the thought of her mother who had passed away just a few months ago from breast cancer. Her mother had been her best friend, her life coach, and her biggest role model, and Faith missed her terribly.

Sabrina Shaw had not allowed an unplanned pregnancy during her second year of college or Faith's father leaving them because he decided fatherhood was not for him to hold her back. Her mother kept right on moving, managing to finish college on time to receive her bachelor's in marketing from New York University, getting a full-time job and then taking evening and online courses for her MBA while raising her child as a single parent. Faith had grown up watching her mother struggle for years to keep a roof over their head and food on the table.

She was her mother's biggest cheerleader when she was finally offered a position as a global marketing manager with a six-figure salary for a top fashion designer. Her mother's success afforded them the opportunity to finally leave their cramped apartment behind and move into a beautiful home in the suburbs so that Faith would be able to live in a neighborhood and attend a high school where she could feel safe. In spite of the money her mother made they continued to live frugally which afforded Faith the opportunity to work straight through her bachelor's in fashion design at Parsons New York campus to her master's in fashion studies at Parsons Paris campus. Faith's mother had not only made her own dreams come true but Faith's as well.

As Faith entered the lobby of the building where she was meeting her lawyer, she spotted him talking to a female security guard who was flirting outrageously with him. She couldn't blame the woman. Ezra was a very good-looking brother who fit the tall, dark, and handsome role perfectly. Not to mention that his perfectly tailored Armani suit, leather loafers, and leather briefcase smelled of money and success.

If she dated men he definitely would have been the type she would go for. Suddenly, a vision of the woman she saw on the train came to mind and it made her smile. She had a sexy self-confidence about her that piqued Faith's interest the moment she saw her, and it was obvious by the way the other woman watched her that her interest was piqued as well.

If the train hadn't been so crowded she would have made her way over to talk. Unfortunately, the train didn't empty until they reached her stop and a quick glance back told her it wasn't the other woman's stop. Faith had waited to see if she would exit the station, but when she didn't spot her she went on her way. It was probably for the best since her life was too complicated right now to even think about dating anyone.

Ezra smiled as he spotted her approaching. "I didn't think you would make it in time," he said as he drew her into a tight embrace.

The disappointment on the security guard's face almost made Faith laugh.

"Well, I did. I may have lost a buyer, but I'm here," she said.

When Ezra moved to release her from the embrace, Faith held on for just a moment longer then let go.

"You okay?" Ezra asked.

"I am now. Just needed one of your healing bear hugs," she said.

"I may have to add healing hugs to my services," he said with a grin.

They were interrupted by the security guard. "If she's going up with you she's going to need a badge," she said in an annoyed tone.

Faith handed the woman her ID and waited patiently for the visitor badge to be made. The guard slid her ID and the badge across the desk to her. Faith smiled pleasantly at the woman and said, "Have wonderful afternoon," getting nothing but an eye roll in response.

"I think I might have just ruined your chances with her," Faith said.

Ezra laughed. "Thank you, because my lack of interest didn't seem to deter her."

"Face it, you've grown into quite an eligible bachelor since high school."

"And I thoroughly enjoy all the benefits that come with that title," he said.

Faith laughed. "I can't wait to see the day some woman comes along and makes you forget all about being a bachelor."

"Unless she can measure up to you then I can't see that happening," he said with an exaggerated sigh.

Faith gave him the same eye roll she had received from the infatuated security guard.

"So what are the evil threesome after today?" Faith asked as they got on the elevator.

Ezra's playful demeanor faded away. "Craig wants to sell the house."

Faith's heart skipped a beat. "Which house?" she asked, already knowing the answer.

"The Glenridge, New Jersey, house."

Faith could feel the tightness in her chest that always came when she had to deal with Craig Lawson and his daughters, Monet and Chenelle.

"No. My mother loved that house, and I won't let that con artist profit from it," she said angrily.

"Since your mother left the house to you he has no claim on it or right to sell it so this shouldn't take long. I would have taken this meeting on my own, but since it's the Glenridge house I knew you would want to be here."

Faith gave Ezra's hand a gentle squeeze. "Thank you."

They reached their destination and entered the offices of the Lawsons' attorney. They were brought to a conference room where Craig, Monet, and Chenelle were waiting with their two attorneys.

Faith didn't like the smug, Cheshire cat grin Craig had on his face. He was up to something, and Faith knew she wasn't going to like it. Next to him sat Monet looking as if she was in serious need of a good meal. If Faith didn't know any better she would swear the already too thin woman had lost even more weight in her determination to become a runway model. Her sister, Chenelle, sat beside her, the complete opposite of Monet's tall skeletal frame, with her short stature and rounded torso. She dreamed of becoming the next Jennifer Hudson. She had the talent; unfortunately, she also had her father as her manager. Under different circumstances Faith thought she and Chenelle could have been good friends. It was too bad her father's and sister's influence over her was stronger than her own self-confidence.

Faith's mother met Craig, a real estate agent, almost three years ago. She was happy for her mother who had spent so much of her life focusing on either Faith's well-being or her career that she rarely made time for a relationship of her own.

Before Craig, the longest meaningful relationship Faith knew her mother had lasted four months and ended because he could no longer handle her mother's work coming before him. Craig had somehow charmed his way not only into her mother's heart but Faith's as well by getting her mother to slow down and relax more. When he asked Faith for her mother's hand in marriage a year later, Faith didn't see any reason why she would disagree. He had told them he was a widow with two daughters he had raised on his own while building his real estate business. He told them his parents had passed some time ago, and that other than his daughters, his only other family was a sister who lived out of the country and some cousins he rarely spoke to. He treated her mother like a queen, never let her pay for anything, seemed to treasure the ground she walked on. The few times Faith had met his daughters before the wedding, they came across as very pleasant. Faith had even liked Chenelle and offered to introduce her to a club owner she and Ezra had grown up with who did open mic nights to help her with her career.

Their lives changed drastically a year later when a mass was found in her mother's left breast. She had not been consistent with her annual appointments and had either ignored or chosen not to tell anyone of any symptoms she was having, so by the time it was discovered it had reached Stage 4, spreading to her lymph nodes. After a mastectomy of her left breast, which included lymph node removal, and four weeks of radiation treatment, her mother was given a clean bill of health. Her mother was not a vain woman so missing a breast didn't worry her as much as not being around for her family.

She took her recovery and post-surgery health seriously, but the very treatment that removed the cancer caused damage to her lungs. Craig had been the wonderfully supportive husband until her mother's health deteriorated to the point where she required an oxygen tank to assist her breathing on a regular basis. He hired a nurse and would disappear for days claiming it was for a business venture he was working on, and when he was home avoided her mother as much as possible.

Faith moved back home to help care for her mother who, in spite of her failing health, stayed in good spirits. A few months before her mother succumbed to her illness, her accountant contacted Faith, who her mother had given power of attorney to for her legal and financial matters, to inform her that Craig had withdrawn twenty thousand dollars from their joint bank account. When Faith told her mother about the missing funds, her mother admitted to Faith that the only thing that surprised her was that he had waited so long to do it. She then told Faith she had learned a year ago that Craig wasn't all that he claimed to be.

The sister that he told them was living in Europe actually lived in North Carolina and had contacted her mother after she heard Craig had gotten married. It seemed Craig had a history of charming wealthy women into relationships then milking them for all he could before getting caught and disappearing when he tired of them. His sister had called to warn her mother and had even given her the names of some of the women she knew Craig had conned into giving him the small fortune he had managed to accumulate before meeting her.

Faith had asked her why she stayed with him after finding out the truth. Her mother told her she believed that in spite of his original goal to con her, Craig must have truly loved her because he had never married any of the other women.

Faith couldn't believe her strong, independent mother could think so naively and told her that very thing. Her mother had laughed and explained that believing in love didn't make her naive. Before she and Craig married she had her attorney and accountant create security restrictions for her finances to ensure any suspicious activity was flagged and she was notified immediately. She set up the joint account with Craig to appease him, but the bulk of her finances were secure. She loved Craig, but she was no fool.

When her mother passed away, Craig reacted with such heartbreak that Faith could almost believe her mother was right about him loving her after all. That lasted all of two weeks before the dollar signs blinded him to whatever he might have felt for her mother and the grieving widower became the smooth con artist once again. The biggest shock to Faith was to find out that Chenelle and Monet knew all along what their father had been doing. When her mother's will was read, she had left everything to Faith. Craig was given stock they had invested in and two properties they purchased during their marriage, as well as what he had left in their joint back account.

Monet was the one who outed them when she had angrily shouted at her father. "Three years and that's all you got out of it for us?" Chenelle had been shocked by her sister's outburst but couldn't hide the look of guilt that followed when Faith looked at her.

"Why do you all insist on wasting everyone's time this way?" Faith asked.

"Because my father deserves more than the pittance your ungrateful mother left him after he stayed with and cared for her when she was sick," Monet said angrily.

"Monet," Chenelle said in warning at the dark look on Faith's face.

"My client did not come here to be, or to have her deceased mother, insulted," Ezra said to the attorney across from him.

The attorney cleared his throat nervously. "Yes, well, let's get on with why we're here. As Mr. Lawson is no longer able to stay in the home he shared with Mrs. Lawson—"

"Ms. Shaw," Ezra corrected him. "She kept her maiden name after marriage."

"Uh, yes, my apologies. Mr. Lawson would like to sell the home as he can no longer bear living there since Ms. Shaw's passing."

"In spite of Mr. Lawson still living at the residence, the property is not his to sell. It was left to my client, and she has generously allowed Mr. Lawson and his daughters to stay there until they are able to find a place of their own," Ezra said.

"Yes, and my client is very appreciative of Miss Shaw's kindness—"

Faith snorted in derision and received a disapproving kick under the table from Ezra.

Craig's attorney glanced at Faith who met his gaze, not the least bit bothered by his stern expression. When he realized he had no effect on her, he turned back to Ezra.

"As it is obvious neither Mr. Lawson nor Miss Shaw are interested in occupying the residence, we see no objection with selling the property. He is, of course, offering to sell the home via his real estate company with Miss Shaw receiving all monies made from the sale with a ten percent commission for Mr. Lawson."

Faith had heard enough. "You're kidding right? You seriously cannot believe this is going to work?" she said to the attorney, then swung her glance toward Craig.

Ezra placed a hand on her arm as she stood. "Faith," he said.

"No, Ezra, I can't sit quietly anymore while this man continues to disrespect my mother and all that she worked for."

Craig looked down, not able to meet Faith's angry gaze. "I loved your mother too," he said.

"You could've fooled me. Where were you that last month when she couldn't walk into another room without needing to drag along her oxygen? Where were you when we sat at the funeral home making arrangements for her own memorial service and cremation? Where were you on that night in the hospital when she took her last breath?" She angrily wiped away tears. "None of you were there for her when she most needed it." Her gaze landed on each of the Lawsons across from her. Monet even had enough heart to look a tad guilty.

Craig looked up, tears glistening unshed in his eyes. "I couldn't watch her waste away like that."

Faith laughed bitterly. "And you think it was easier for me to do so? That was my mother…MY MOTHER! Not some rich gullible broad for you to swindle. And don't think she didn't know. She knew all about you and she still loved you. If this is what you do to people you love, use them until they're no longer of use to you, I feel sorry for you."

Faith picked up her bag. "I will not be selling my mother's home, and I want all of you vacated from the house within the next three weeks."

"But we have nowhere else to go!" Chenelle said, speaking for the first time since Faith walked into the room.

"You should have thought of that before taking my mother's generosity for granted. If it had been up to me you would have been gone the day after her funeral," Faith said before walking out of the office with Ezra following behind.

They stood quietly waiting for the elevator, Faith doing her best to keep it together. As soon as the elevator doors closed, hot tears rolled down her cheeks. Ezra wrapped an arm around her waist and pulled her close. She laid her head on his shoulder with a shuddering sigh.

He placed a soft kiss on her forehead. "Your mother would've been proud at how maturely you handled that."

"Thanks, Ez. Can you do me one last favor?"

Ezra nodded. "Anything."

"Please make sure they're gone before I get back from Turks and Caicos. I don't know if I'll be able to be so mature again if I come back from spreading Momma's ashes to find them still there."

"Will do," he said, giving her a quick squeeze before the elevator opened and they walked out into the lobby.

Cass sat back in the lounge chair on her private veranda listening to the demo of an artist Ebony had brought to her attention, and she could see why. The young woman was raw and reminded her a lot of Ebony's early music. Like Ebony, she could sing and did her own hooks as well. Cass hit the pause button and jotted down notes in the notebook she carried on her at all times. Cass was old-fashioned that way, writing everything down. Ebony told her she needed to get one of those electronic notebook apps and just record her notes there, but there was something about feeling the pen in her hand, hearing it scratch across the paper as she wrote, and the crisp sound of the pages turning as she read back her notes that gave her a sense of comfort.

Besides, writing relaxed her, which is what she was supposed to be doing right now instead of working. She looked out past the end of her veranda to where white sandy beach and clear blue waters lay, and all she could think of was the work that would be waiting for her when she got back to the office at the end of the week. Ebony and Stephanie had conspired and practically had her kidnapped to get her here. Cass had to admit they pulled a good one over on her. She had suffered a serious migraine after a three-hour meeting with battling artists Frenetic and Cree where they now had to arrange different studio time slots to get their collaboration finished in time for the album release. It was so bad Ebony had to take her home and put her to bed like some sick child. Cass was laid up for two days. Two days in which Ebony and Stephanie began their conspiring.

When she got back to work, Ebony insisted they had to fly to Atlanta the next day to check out some underground rap artist. When Cass insisted Ebony go alone this one time she wouldn't hear of it. Said it would save them the time of having to make two separate trips. She even offered to get a private jet to fly them there and back same day so Cass wouldn't miss any more work. Cass gave in. Ebony told her she would meet her at the airport first thing in the morning. Cass got to Teterboro Airport and boarded the jet Ebony had reserved for them and got comfortable to wait for her.

Ten minutes later, she got a text from Ebony telling her to "Enjoy your vacation" with a winking smiley face. Confused, Cass called Ebony instead of responding to the text. Just as Ebony answered, the flight attendant shut the door, smiled sweetly at her, and asked her to buckle her seat belt before disappearing into the front of the cabin.

"What the hell is going on, Eb?" she had asked.

Ebony chuckled. "You're taking an impromptu and well-deserved vacation. Try and relax, Cass. Stephanie and I have everything taken care of here."

Then to Cass's chagrin, Ebony had hung up.

Cass stared at her phone for a good five minutes before she realized the plane had begun its taxi down the runway. She sent one last text before takeoff to both Ebony and Stephanie threatening to fire them as soon as she got back from God knew where they were sending her to, then angrily slammed her phone down on the table. That's when she looked at a folder that had been on the table when she sat down but she had ignored until now. She opened it and found a note from Stephanie.

Since you insist on working yourself to death, we figured you should enjoy at least one week of sun and fun before you

do. Don't worry, Ebony and I can handle whatever comes up.
Pure Music will still be here when you get back. We're only
doing this because we love you.

—Stephanie

Attached to the note was an itinerary with nothing but the word RELAX under each day of the schedule. Nothing telling her where she was going, which was not good for someone who always had to be in control of every situation. Once the plane was airborne, the flight attendant greeted her again with a mimosa, introduced herself, and told her breakfast would be served shortly. Cass tried to ask her where they were going, but she only suggested she sit back and relax; everything had been taken care of. Since it was obvious everyone was in on this plan but her, Cass reluctantly stopped trying to figure out what was going on because it had only given her a headache.

After breakfast, Cass fell asleep and was awakened by the flight attendant notifying her that they would be landing soon. She looked at her watch and realized she had slept for three hours. When she looked out the window she was greeted by white sand and clear blue water.

As she left the plane, the flight attendant handed her a rolling suitcase she recognized as her own that Stephanie must have packed for her, and told her to have a wonderful trip and that they would be here to take her home at the end of the week. At the bottom of the stairs, there was another attendant who welcomed her to Turks and Caicos, then escorted her to a waiting car at the entrance of the airport.

When she arrived at the resort she was greeted by Serge, her own personal butler for the week, who escorted her to a beachfront villa she had all to herself. This was her second out of the seven days she was supposed to be here, and she still couldn't believe Ebony and Stephanie had pulled all this off in a matter of days. After her massage this morning, she had grudgingly sent them a thank you via text and told them that maybe she wouldn't fire them after all when she got back.

Cass looked back down at her notes. Maybe she was working too hard. Here she was steps away from one of the most beautiful beaches in the world, and she hadn't stepped a foot onto it. Not giving herself a chance to change her mind, Cass went to the bedroom, put her notebook away, changed into a pair of turquoise and white floral print board shorts, a white cropped short sleeved fitted swim top, white and turquoise water shoes, and a pair of aviator sunglasses, and then grabbed a rolled beach mat Stephanie had managed to fit into her luggage. Cass realized after Serge had unpacked her luggage and put everything neatly in its place that her assistant was due for a raise. Not only had she packed the perfect outfits, accessories, toiletries, and other items Cass would not have thought of herself, she also fit it efficiently into one suitcase. Cass was in the kitchenette grabbing a bottle of water to take with her when Serge knocked on the door.

"Good morning, Miss Cass. I was just stopping by to see if you will be having lunch in your room again, but it looks like you're going to head out to the beach."

"Good morning, Serge. Yeah, I figured since I'm forced to take a vacation I might as well enjoy it."

"Sounds like a good plan to me. Can I get you anything? I will be happy to set up your lunch on the beach."

"Wow, you would do that?"

"Yes, it comes with the package your friends kindly gifted you," he said. "I can set it up on the sands close to your villa. If you let me know what you would like I can make sure it's available at the time you would like."

She had just eaten a light breakfast of fruit, granola, and yogurt about an hour ago. "I'll do lunch about twelve thirty, and why don't you surprise me. I usually don't have time to really eat lunch when I'm working. I have no food allergies and I love seafood and chicken."

Serge nodded. "I'm sure I can come up with something you will enjoy. I will see you then. In the meantime enjoy your walk."

"Thanks, Serge." Cass grabbed her water bottle and headed out the veranda door.

The strip of beach Cass walked along wasn't as crowded as she expected. She wasn't sure if it was because there were mostly private villas along the area or because it was the end of the high season, whatever the reason, she found she didn't mind. It was actually a relief from the noise and crowds of New York City. She could see why so many of her associates bought property in the Caribbean to escape the rat race. When she got home she was going to have to talk to her attorney about looking into some properties. Cass found a nice spot to stop and sit for a bit before she headed back to see what Serge managed to have thrown together for her lunch. She laid her mat down on the sand under an unoccupied grass umbrella and watched a family frolicking in the water.

Movement to the right of the family caught her eye as someone swam into view. As the person emerged from the water and walked toward the shore, Cass's eyes widened in surprise. It was the woman from the subway walking toward the shore like a vision from an erotic dream. At that moment, dressed in a swimsuit, Cass thought the African goddess title she had given her when she'd first seen her on the train fit perfectly.

As the woman stopped at a low beach chair about five feet from where Cass sat, she grabbed a towel and began drying herself off. Cass found she couldn't tear her eyes away. The goddess filled out her bathing suit very well. The halter top cupped a set of generously full breasts above a small waist; the high cut leg outlined her long, shapely legs, and the bottom portion of the suit barely covered a generous, round behind. Cass took her time admiring the lush curves. As someone who spent a lot of time in the gym, Cass could tell by her tight body and muscles that the goddess did as well but not so much that it took away her feminine curves and softness. As her gaze made its way back up, it connected with the goddess's full, lush-lipped smile and hypnotic, deep brown eyes. Cass realized she had been caught checking her out and grinned sheepishly, but she didn't let her gaze drop from the other woman's.

"Have we met?" the woman called over.

"Uh, no," Cass said in surprise, not having expected the goddess to speak to her. She stood and began walking toward her. Play it cool, she said to herself as she slowed her gait into a cool saunter.

As she walked over, Faith took that moment to check the other woman out. She had a smooth, golden bronze complexion and wavy jet-black hair cropped into a fade. She wore sunglasses, but Faith vividly remembered connecting to the brilliant hazel eyes beneath. She was a good six feet tall with a muscular build and tight swim shirt that emphasized small rounded breasts and a taut six-pack of abs. Faith could tell by the way the other woman's shapely mouth turned up into a cocky grin that she liked the way Faith was boldly checking her out and liking what she saw.

"I believe we took the same train once." Cass offered her hand. "I'm Cass," she said in introduction.

Faith smiled. "Hello, Cass, I'm Faith." She grasped the offered hand.

"Small world that we would also end up on the same stretch of beach on a Caribbean island. Do you believe in fate, Cass?" Faith said, reluctantly releasing Cass's hand.

"I believe in coincidence, and I would say this was a lucky coincidence," Cass responded.

"Lucky for you or me?" Faith asked flirtatiously.

With a mock serious expression Cass responded, "Let's see, if I said lucky for you, then I would sound very cocky. If I said lucky for me, then that would sound like a pickup line. How about we're both lucky to be on this beautiful island paradise instead of an overcrowded subway car."

"I can't argue with that. Well, I won't take up more of your island time. It was a pleasure meeting you, Cass. Maybe we'll see each other again on the train."

Cass gently grasped Faith's fingers and, keeping her eyes locked with Faith's, raised them to her lips and pressed a soft kiss on her knuckles.

"I'll be sure to look for you. It was a pleasure meeting you as well," she said, then gently lowered and released Faith's hand before turning to walk away.

"Cass," Faith called.

Cass turned back to Faith.

"I was just going to the restaurant to have lunch. Would you like to join me?" Faith assumed, judging by the solo setup she had under the grass umbrella, that Cass was traveling alone.

"Actually, I have lunch being set up at my room if you'd like to join me there," Cass offered.

Faith quirked her eyebrow questioningly.

"You'll be perfectly safe. It's being set up on the beach in front of my villa," she quickly explained.

Faith held back an amused smile at Cass's discomfort. "That sounds much more inviting than the restaurant. I'd be happy to join you."

"Great, let me just grab my things and we'll head there," Cass turned and headed back to her beach set up.

Faith took a moment to admire Cass's backside as she jogged toward the umbrella, then quickly turned to put the few things she had brought with her into her beach bag. When she recognized Cass as the woman from the train, her flirtatious side decided to rear its coquettish little head, especially since she had thought about her frequently since then. The fact that it made an appearance today, of all days, was interesting.

"Momma, I don't have time for you to be playing match-maker from heaven," she said as she put on her swimsuit cover up.

"Ready?" Cass asked as she walked over.

"Lead the way," Faith said.

"It's just a five-minute walk from here. Plenty of time for you to change your mind," Cass joked.

"Just to warn you, I have a black belt in tae kwon do and recently completed a Krav Maga self-defense class."

Cass whistled. "Impressive. I've been training in mixed martial arts for about a year now. Helps relieve stress."

"That's a pretty aggressive stress reliever."

"I get pretty aggressive stress."

"Is that same stress that brought you here?" Faith asked.

"I guess it is. This trip wasn't planned, at least not by me," Cass said, sounding a bit annoyed.

Faith's step hesitated. "Oh, are you here with someone who planned it?" she asked. Did she misread Cass's flirting and lunch invitation?

"No, I'm here alone. My assistant and one of my coworkers decided I needed a vacation and had me hijacked here."

"Seriously?" Faith asked in surprise.

"Seriously," Cass said.

Faith laughed. "You had to be hijacked into going on vacation to Turks and Caicos?"

Cass looked down with an embarrassed smile.

Faith shook her head in disbelief. "I guess you really do stress aggressively."

"So I guess you don't have to be strong-armed into going on vacation," Cass said.

"My mother and I used to rent a private villa here every year," Faith said, sadness tingeing her voice.

"Used to?" Cass asked.

Faith gazed quietly ahead for a moment. "My mother passed away several months ago."

Cass's steps halted. "I'm sorry to hear that."

"She had been sick a long time so it wasn't unexpected. I'm actually here for one of her final wishes to have her ashes spread here on the island."

Faith started walking again and Cass followed. "Have you already spread her ashes?"

"Not yet. Tonight at midnight. Tomorrow is her birthday," Faith said.

Cass frowned and Faith looped her arm around Cass's. "It's really okay. I'm fine. I had just been thinking I really didn't want to be alone today and then you showed up."

"Really?"

Faith smiled. "Really."

They resumed their stroll in companionable silence. A short time later, Cass spotted Serge on a spot of beachfront in front of her villa setting an umbrella table. He looked up as they drew closer and his eyes widened in surprise. Cass wondered what he could be thinking; she'd only been there two days, and her first day out of the room she brought someone home.

"Faith?" Serge said, walking toward them with his arms outstretched.

Faith released Cass's arm and walked into Serge's embrace.

"Serge, it's so good to see you!" Faith said.

"You two know each other?" Cass asked in confusion.

Chuckling, Faith stepped back and grasped Serge's hands. "Serge and I are old friends. He's taken care of my mom and me since we started coming here."

"I was so sad to hear about her passing," Serge said.

"I brought her with me for a final good-bye if you and your mom would like to join me tonight. I had planned to call your mom later today to let her know," Faith said.

"We would be honored," he said with unshed tears sparkling in his eyes.

Faith wiped a tear away before it could escape the corner of her eye. "I'm glad. It will be at midnight at the property."

"Will you be joining Miss Cass for lunch?" Serge asked.

"Yes, she will," Cass answered.

"Excellent. I will get another place setting."

"Thank you Serge," Cass said.

Cass walked over to the table and spotted a small cooler. She opened it to find Serge had supplied her with her favorite beer, a bottle of white wine, and bottled water.

"Can I offer you something to drink?" Cass asked Faith.

Faith looked over her shoulder at the contents of the cooler. "I'll take a bottle of water for now."

Cass handed her a bottle and picked up a beer for herself then offered Faith the lone seat. Serge returned shortly with another chair and place setting.

"Your lunch should be brought up shortly," he offered.

"Thank you again, Serge."

Cass watched him leave then turned her attention back to Faith. "So you weren't kidding when you said you were here every year."

"Yeah, we started coming to Turks and Caicos when I was about sixteen, and we met Serge and his mom at a smaller resort where they were working. He was actually the one who suggested we start coming to this resort several years ago when they left the other one to start working here. His mom is the director of housekeeping and Serge is head butler. He and his mother are planning to open their own bed and breakfast on the island."

"So you all are close?" Cass asked.

"It started with our moms chatting it up and eventually they became good friends over the years. Serge and I ended up becoming friends by association." Faith took a sip of her water.

"So, when you're not being tricked into going on vacation what do you do?" Faith asked.

"I'm a music producer," Cass answered, which was partially the truth. She didn't think Faith would be one of those girls who only saw dollar signs when Cass told them she owned a recording label, but she didn't want to take that chance. "What about you? What do you do?"

"Shoe designer," Faith answered.

"Really? What brand do you work for?" Cass asked.

"None. I have a little boutique and design studio in Jersey City. I'm trying to find an independent distributor to get my own shoe line in the major stores. Until then, I'm very happy with my boutique and doing custom orders. When you're back home you should stop by my shop and studio." Faith reached for her bag, pulled out her card case, and handed a business card to Cass.

It was a white card with a drawing of a glass stiletto shoe on a red pillow. "Glass Slippers by Faith," Cass read.

"Yeah, it's a take on Cinderella's glass slipper. It was one of my favorite fairy tales," Faith said. "Don't let the picture fool you. I do all kinds of shoes, from stilettos to flip-flops," she said, lifting her foot to show off her platform flip-flops.

Cass gently grasped Faith's foot to get a better look at the shoe. The heel was a platform wedge made to look like sandblasted wood with turquoise rhinestones, wood beads, and shells along the wide leather thong. She couldn't help but also notice Faith's smooth feet and French manicured toenails. She softly ran her hand up Faith's ankle and calf as she lowered her leg and didn't miss the quick intake of breath from Faith as she did so.

Cass grinned knowingly. The moment was interrupted by Serge bringing their lunch. He rolled a cart with covered dishes and stopped just where the lawn and sand met. He placed dishes in front of each of them, then whisked the covers away to reveal a plate of conch salad and lobster tail, then placed another dish in the middle of the table with slices of mango, melon, and pineapple chunks.

"Bon appetite," Serge said with a bow. "I'll be nearby if you require any further assistance."

"Everything is lovely," Faith said.

"Thank you, Serge," Cass said.

They brought their attention back to their food. Cass reached for serving utensils. "Would you like some fruit?" she asked.

"Yes, please."

Cass placed several slices of the fruit on Faith's plate before serving herself. The courtesy made Faith smile.

"Thank you," she said.

They focused their attention on their food for a few minutes.

"So you're a music producer? Do you work with a particular label or independently?" Faith asked.

"I work strictly with Pure Music Records. Have you heard of them?" Cass said.

"Some of my favorite artists are from that label. The group Charity, gospel singer Frank Lazarus, and of course The Beast."

Cass gazed at Faith in surprise. "I would have never pegged you as a 'Beast Monger,'" she said, using the nickname Ebony's fans had labeled themselves.

"The single 'Retribution' got me through a really tough time in my teen years.

"Oh you thought that you could break me
But your demons have remade me
Into something that should not be
I won't fight the beast within me
The Devil even fears me
When I rain down retribution"

"Check you out," Cass said, impressed that she knew the verses from one of Ebony's lesser played singles. It had been one of her underground hits that Pure Music decided to record for her first album. Unfortunately, it didn't get much airtime because the stations believed it was too hardcore to add to their regular rotation. Ebony had refused to record a radio edit version so the only ones who really knew the single were diehard Beast fans because they had the albums.

"Don't let the pretty face fool you. There's a little thug under all of this glamour," Faith said with a wink.

Cass laughed. "All right, Miss Thug, I'll have to remember not to get on your bad side."

"Did you start out as a hip-hop artist also?"

"No, but I've always been around music. My mother is a piano teacher and my father is a session musician playing bass guitar and drums for studio recording sessions. I spent a lot of summers in the studio with him," Cass answered.

"Do you play any instruments?"

"Yeah, piano, drums, and bass guitar, but I was more fascinated with the technical and production aspect of recording music rather than making it. I actually started out making a name for myself as a club DJ which is how I ended up in New York. I met the CEO of Pure Music at a club one night, made some suggestions on how I could help give her artists a better sound, and instead of kicking me to the curb she brought me to the studio for a session with Ebony Trent, liked what I did, and I've been there ever since," Cass explained. She intentionally left out becoming president and CEO of the label. "Now it's your turn," Cass said. "Tell me how you got into the shoe game."

Faith grabbed a beer from the cooler Serge left them.

Cass smiled. Faith appeared to be the epitome of style and sophistication yet she was quoting hardcore rap music and preferred beer instead of the wine Serge provided for them.

"My favorite book to read with my mother was *Cinderella* and she loved shoes, so one Christmas when I was about six years old I decided to make her very own pair of glass slippers like Cinderella. I broke into my piggy bank and recruited my grandmother to help me purchase a pair of plain inexpensive pumps and some stick-on rhinestones from the craft store. I spent a week every day after school at my grandmother's house carefully placing rhinestones over every inch of those shoes to make them look like glass slippers." Faith smiled.

"They were the gaudiest pair of shoes, but my mother loved them. She wore them the entire day as well as to church on Sunday bragging to everyone how I had made them and that I would be a famous shoe designer one day. Then for my birthday she bought me a sketch pad, art pencils, a one-hundred-dollar gift card for a local craft store, and about ten pairs of those five-dollar hanger sneakers from some discount store so I could create my own custom shoes. I'm where I am today because of her and I miss her so much," Faith said, tears escaping from the corner of her eyes.

Cass's heart broke a little at the heartache in Faith's eyes. She grasped her hand and gave it a comforting squeeze. She'd just met this woman yet she somehow was feeling her pain as if it were her own. Faith wiped her tears with her napkin and gave Cass a smile in gratitude for her comfort.

"Okay, no more weepiness. Let's enjoy this delicious lunch." Faith gave Cass's hand a squeeze in return before releasing it to grab her fork.

After a few minutes of eating Faith asked "So there's no one special in your life that would have loved to have been kidnapped to go on vacation with you?"

"No. I honestly don't have much time for a social life, which is why my assistant and Ebony had to have me hijacked for a vacation."

"I know the feeling. I'm working practically twenty of a twenty-four-hour day trying to keep my boutique open, expand my locations, and find distributors so I guess you can say I was somewhat hijacked to come here per my mother's final wishes because I would not have taken my vacation this year if it weren't for that," Faith said.

"So I guess that means there's no one special in your life?" Cass asked, trying not to sound too hopeful.

"No. I haven't even gone on a date in at least a year," Faith said with a chuckle.

Cass's eyes widened in surprise. "Really?"

"Really. A friend of mine has tried fixing me up with a coworker and a couple of musician friends of his, but they were a disaster. The last one was a high profile attorney who spent most of the date talking about herself and her celebrity clients and answering calls. I promised myself right then and there that, one, I wouldn't let anymore friends set me up on dates, and two, I would stay away from celebrities and women with high-profile careers. I'm already playing second fiddle to my career. I don't want to be second fiddle to someone else's, and I'm not good with being in the spotlight. I don't even use my own image on anything to do with Glass Slippers except my name," Faith said.

Cass was now glad she hadn't told Faith what she really did. It wasn't a lot, but she did spend time in the spotlight often enough. "I could understand that. Because of the business I'm in I end up dating people who are also in the industry, in front of and behind the mic, but I do my best not to mix business with pleasure."

"You've never dated an artist you've worked with?" Faith asked.

"Yes, and it ended badly," Cass said with a frown remembering all the media attention around the breakup and the lawyers that had to get involved when her ex started spreading false accusations about Cass harassing and stalking her when it was the other way around.

"No one since then?" Faith asked.

"Not seriously," Cass responded.

Faith reached for two bottles of beer from the cooler placing one in front of Cass and the other for herself. "We seem to have a lot in common. Serial single workaholics with no social life."

"Some of the best relationships have started with less."

"True. Do you have plans for dinner?" Faith asked.

"I was hoping you were available."

"As a matter of fact I am. I know a spot that my mother and I used to go to."

"An evening on a tropical island with a beautiful stranger at an unknown location, how could I say no," Cass said with a smile.

"Great, then it's a date." Faith took one last healthy swig from her beer and stood.

"I'll swing by at seven to pick you up. Thank you for lunch." Faith leaned over and placed a soft kiss on Cass's cheek then headed back the way they had come.

Cass watched the sexy sway of her full hips as Faith disappeared around a cluster of bushes toward a path leading to other villas in the area.

"Would you like me to clear away lunch, miss?" Serge asked, startling Cass who hadn't realized he had walked up to the table.

"Uh, yes, thank you, and, Serge, you can just call me Cass," she said with a smile.

Serge smiled in return. "You're welcome, Cass."

Cass picked up her unfinished beer and headed into the villa. Just as she sat on the sofa, her phone vibrated in her pocket. Ebony's name flashed on the screen.

"Everything all right?" she asked, assuming the worst.

Ebony chuckled on the other end. "Damn, bro, everything is fine. I was just calling to check on you."

Cass sighed in relief. "You wouldn't have to call and check on me if you hadn't had me kidnapped in the first place. I need to be there handling business not lounging on the beach."

"Cass, you know you needed a break just as much as we knew you needed one. We need you recharged and at one hundred percent for the ball and the upcoming tours. Besides, there is nothing going on here that Stephanie and I can't handle."

"I guess," Cass said begrudgingly.

"So how's island life treating you?" Ebony asked.

"It's good. I'm thinking of investing in property here. Maybe some place I could build a private recording studio," Cass responded.

"That sounds like a good idea. Have you contacted any Realtors yet?"

"No, but I plan on doing that tomorrow. In the meantime, can you do me a favor? Would you please have Stephanie create a file for Glass Slippers by Faith and email it to me ASAP."

"Glass Slippers by Faith? Isn't that a boutique in Jersey? Belinda shops there sometimes," Ebony told her.

"Does she know the owner?" Cass asked.

"Yeah, why? What's up?"

"Nothing's up. I happened to meet the owner, Faith, today and I was curious about the business."

"The business or the woman?"

"Eb, can you just have Stephanie run the check for me?"

Ebony laughed. "I got you, bro. Enjoy the rest of your vacay."

"Yeah, thanks," Cass said with a grin before hanging up.

Cass thought about Ebony and how she had been through hell and back and managed to find someone to love her, to tame The Beast. There shouldn't be any reason Cass couldn't find the same thing.

❖

Faith stood in front of her mirror in the third dress she had tried on in the past ten minutes. All three were dresses she had bought that afternoon after setting up her date with Cass. She couldn't decide which she liked best so she did something she never did, she bought all three. She had not planned on going out during this trip so she had only brought casual wear, nothing dressy or formal. They weren't going any place fancy, and she could have just worn one of her simple sundresses, but for some reason she felt the need to dress up a little for Cass, for her first date in a year. The dress she had on was a sleeveless long flowing buttercup yellow maxi dress made from a soft jersey material. The front of the dress had a modest V-neckline that settled just at the start of her cleavage and a slit up the right leg that hit just above her knee. She did a little turn and looked over her shoulder at the open back of the dress which dipped to her lower back just below her rib cage.

"The third try is the charm," she said to herself, deciding on wearing the dress and returning the other two dresses tomorrow.

She looked at the small shoe collection she had brought with her. She always traveled with more shoes than she needed because she believed it was always more difficult finding the right pair of shoes at the last minute than it was the right dress. She decided on a pair of pointed toe red stilettos that laced up her ankle.

She gave herself a final look in the mirror then, after a quick dab of scented oil behind her ears and at her cleavage, headed out of her bedroom before she changed her mind again. She decided to walk over to Cass's villa, then they would walk to the main lobby of the resort where the vehicle she rented would be waiting for them.

❖

Cass took one final look at herself in the mirror and walked out to the living area of her villa to wait for Faith. She was so glad Stephanie had packed for her. She had found a pair of black linen pants and an ivory linen jacket in her wardrobe which had somehow either managed to survive the packing without wrinkling or Serge had had her clothes pressed before hanging them up when he unpacked for her. She paired the pants and jacket with a black silk T-shirt and a pair of black canvas slip-on shoes. At her request, Serge had sent a barber to her room earlier to tighten up her cut. She paced around the living room full of nervous energy wondering why this woman was having such a strong effect on her.

There was a knock on the door, and Cass practically jumped out of her skin. She looked through the peephole. Serge stood smiling on the other side of the door. Cass almost sighed in relief as she opened it.

"Hey, Serge." She stepped aside to let him in.

"Good evening, Cass. I just wanted to check in to see if there's anything else you may need for the evening."

"No, I'm heading out to dinner with Faith so I'm good," Cass said.

Serge's smile broadened. "I'll just straighten up a bit and do the turndown service, then I will see you in the morning."

"Thank you, Serge."

Serge nodded then headed for the bedroom. "Oh, Cass," he said.

Cass turned to meet his smiling gaze. "I think you two are good match. Have a wonderful evening," he said and went on about his work.

Cass smiled. "Thanks, Serge."

A few moments later, there was another knock on her door. Cass was no longer as nervous, but she still felt a slight fluttering mix of nervous excitement in her belly as she opened the door.

"Hi," Faith said with a broad smile.

"Hi," Cass responded. "You look beautiful and the shoes are sexy as hell."

To Faith's surprise, she felt her cheeks heat in a blush. "Thank you. You look great as well. Ready to go?"

"Thank you. Yes, let me just grab my wallet and room key," Cass said, grabbing both from a nearby credenza.

They left Cass's villa, walking toward the main building of the resort.

"I rented a car," Faith told her.

"Oh, do you usually rent a car when you're here?" Cass asked.

"Yes. When we traveled my mom hated depending on taxis or shuttles. She liked to come and go as she pleased. To explore areas of wherever we were visiting as if we were natives," Faith explained.

"Seems like your mother was a free spirit," Cass said.

Faith smiled. "She was. Before she got sick she planned to retire here. That's why her final wishes were for her ashes to be spread at a plot of land she purchased and was planning to build a house on."

"Sounds like she had everything planned out," Cass said.

"She did. She didn't want my grandparents and me to have to make all of these decisions so she and the family lawyer made all her end of life arrangements several months before she passed."

Cass grasped Faith's hand, giving it a gentle squeeze. Faith smiled gratefully and interlocked her fingers with Cass's. They continued their walk hand in hand. When they reached the resort lobby, they stopped at the concierge desk where Faith picked up a set of keys. Then they made their way out the entrance. The only vehicle waiting was a red Jeep Wrangler Sport which they were heading toward. Faith hit the button to unlock the doors.

She chuckled at the surprise on Cass face. "Not quite the vehicle you expected?"

Cass laughed. "No."

"I told you, don't let the pretty face fool you," she said with a wink.

Cass grinned.

Faith turned on the radio to find Bob Marley crooning "Don't worry about a thing…" She smiled. Her mother was definitely with her tonight and seemed to be sending her a message through her favorite song. She briefly looked over at Cass who seemed very relaxed with her head back on the seat, eyes closed, mouthing the words to the song. She turned her eyes back to the road and silently thanked whatever stars aligned themselves tonight to place Cass in her path today of all days when she truly needed the distraction. If it hadn't been for their chance meeting she would have sat in her room until it was time to complete her task, wallowing in sadness and self-pity over having to say good-bye to her mother one final time.

It was a short drive to the restaurant, but by the time they reached their destination Faith felt like every bit of stress and tension she had collected over the past few months had simply drifted away with the island breeze. She exited the car, walked over to Cass, and took her hand.

"Hungry?"

"I could eat," Cass said with a grin.

When they reached the hostess, Faith asked for a table outside. They were seated on a beachside outdoor patio under a palm tree. A live Caribbean music band played, and the ocean was just steps away from where they sat.

"You don't get to relax much, do you?" Faith asked.

"Is it that obvious?" Cass said.

"Just in the difference from the woman I met earlier to the one sitting across from me now. I could see the tension and stress in the tight way you held yourself earlier. Now your whole demeanor has changed. You look like you're finally on a real vacation instead of a forced sabbatical," Faith said.

"Maybe I needed some divine intervention and the fates sent you my way."

"Maybe," Faith said with a soft smile.

"What would you recommend?" Cass asked, looking over the menu.

"Definitely start with the traditional conch salad then either the snapper or lobster. They do both very well," Faith answered.

When their server arrived, Faith ordered a glass of wine, the conch salad, and grilled shrimp. Cass ordered a beer, the conch salad, and grilled snapper. Their drinks arrived quickly and Cass asked about Faith's business as they waited for their food. Cass listened attentively and smiled at the joy that lit up Faith's eyes when she discussed her work. Cass's mother always told her that if you're passionate about what you do then it doesn't feel like work. Most of the time she felt that way about Pure Music. Of course there were days when she wondered if she had made the right decision in taking it over, but she realized that those were the days Ebony and Stephanie tried to tell her she was trying to take on too much and needed to let the people she hired do their jobs.

As if reading her mind, Faith said, "I try to keep a balance between the creative and business aspects of what I do so that I don't get overwhelmed. It's hard sometimes, but I have a good team to help keep me on track."

"Maybe you can teach me a thing or two. I feel like I spend more time putting out fires than I do in the studio," Cass complained.

"As a producer, isn't most of your work in the studio? Doesn't Pure Music have a business team to handle the day-to-day stuff?" Faith asked.

Cass gulped a swallow of beer. She had forgotten that she hadn't told Faith she wasn't just a producer at Pure Music. "Uh, yeah, but there's still budgets and negotiations that have to get done."

Faith nodded. "I see. I guess that would keep you out of the studio especially when signing new artists."

Their food arrived and they enjoyed their dinner for several moments. Faith broke the lull in the conversation by asking Cass about her family.

"I come from a pretty close-knit family. I'm an only child, but I was raised with a dozen cousins who are more like siblings than cousins. My mom has a brother and a sister, and my father has four brothers. Both sets of my grandparents are still kicking. As a matter of fact, we have a ninetieth birthday party coming up for my dad's mom. What about your family?"

"My mother raised me on her own so I don't know my father's family. She has a brother and both of her parents are still around as well. She remarried shortly before she got sick, but he turned out to be a con man so we don't speak."

"Sorry to hear that. My mom's brother is our family's black sheep so we don't really keep in touch with him because of some things he's done. Unfortunately, he's dragged my cousins into some of his schemes as well," she said with a frown. "I hope the guy didn't cause your mom too much trouble."

"No, but he's giving me quite a bit of it."

"I know a great attorney if you need one," Cass offered.

"Thank you, I appreciate the offer, but our family attorney is handling things very well."

They spent the remainder of the dinner and dessert getting to know more about each other's childhoods, likes and dislikes, and skimmed over their dating histories.

Cass's spoon clattered to her plate as she sat back and patted her full stomach. "Wow, I don't think I could eat another bite of food the rest of the night."

Faith chuckled. "Yeah, I think I'll be doing an extra mile on my run in the morning."

"Why don't I get the bill and we take a walk along the beach before we head out," Cass suggested.

"I'd like that," Faith said.

Cass signaled their server to pay the bill. Once that was taken care of, they removed their shoes and Cass stood, offering her hand to Faith. "Shall we?"

Faith laid her hand in Cass's and stood.

"Thank you for agreeing to have dinner with me," Cass said, then turned and led Faith away from the table toward where the patio and beach met.

They walked quietly hand in hand along the shore to where they were far enough along the beach to still see the restaurant but also have a bit of privacy. They halted and looked out toward the horizon. Cass moved to stand behind Faith, wrapping her arms around Faith's waist, clasping them at her belly. Faith entwined her fingers with Cass's.

"I hope I'm not being to forward," Cass said.

"Not at all."

They stood that way for a few more minutes, then Cass placed her lips near Faith's ear. "Ever since I saw you on the subway I haven't been able to stop thinking about you, and then there you were on the beach this afternoon as if I had conjured you up from a dream."

"Maybe you did conjure me and this is all a dream."

Cass placed a soft kiss upon Faith's earlobe. "If it is then I don't ever want to wake up."

Faith turned in Cass's arms, leaned forward, and placed her lips upon Cass's.

Cass tightened her arms around Faith's waist as Faith pulled her closer. The kiss deepened as Cass felt Faith's fingers glide along the nape of her neck, gently massaging. Cass slid her hands along Faith's back settling along the curve of her behind then she pulled Faith's hips towards hers so that their bodies meshed together as one.

After a few moments, Cass slowly brought their kiss to an end, laying her forehead against Faith's. Both were breathing as if they had just finished a sprint.

"Wow," Faith said breathlessly.

"Wow is right."

"Then why did you stop?" Faith asked.

"Because if I hadn't we would be lying out on this beach giving everyone a show."

"Oh, I guess that's a good reason."

Cass placed a soft kiss on Faith's forehead then stepped back just enough to wrap her arm around Faith's waist and steer them back along the path they were walking. Faith placed her arm around Cass's waist and laid her head on Cass's shoulder. They walked for a while longer, then Cass's phone chirped. Without stopping, she pulled it out of her pocket and, seeing who the message was from, shoved her phone back into her jacket pocket without responding.

"If you need to take care of that I don't mind," Faith told her.

"It's nothing that can't wait."

"Are you sure?"

"Positive, although we should probably start heading back. I don't want to make you late meeting Serge and his mother for your mother's farewell," Cass said.

Faith was touched by Cass's consideration. "I know we just met today and it's probably a weird thing to ask on a first date, but would you like to join us? I think you and my mom would have really liked each other so I'm sure she won't mind if you're there."

Cass smiled. "I'd like to be there for you."

Faith steered them back the way they came. "It's just fifteen minutes from here. I wanted to get there a little early anyway to set up."

They made their way back to the restaurant, hopped into the jeep, and Faith drove them a short distance away to an area called Grace Bay Beach. She drove up a lengthy stretch of rocky road to a vacant beachfront lot.

"I see why you got the jeep. Anything less than a four-wheel drive wouldn't have made it up that path," Cass said as they came to a stop steps away from the beach.

"Yeah, and I wasn't going to attempt to trek the path in the dark on foot," Faith said as she got out and walked toward the back of the vehicle.

She opened the hatch and began unloading. Cass helped her, pulling out some tiki torches, a folding table, folding chairs, a Bluetooth speaker, a cake, plates, cups and utensils, and a bottle of sparkling cider. Following Faith's instructions, Cass helped to set up the area for what Faith said was her mother's birthday farewell celebration. By the time they had everything set up, another car was pulling up toward them. A few moments later, they were joined by Serge and his mother, whose name Cass learned was Nadine.

Right at midnight, their small service began with each telling their favorite story about Faith's mother. Faith told the Cinderella shoe story and had even brought the shoes which had been in a box in the back seat with her mother's ashes, then Nadine told her story about how she and Faith's mother met, and Serge finished with his story about Faith's mother encouraging him to get his business degree and even helping to pay his tuition.

After the stories were told, Faith led the small entourage to the shoreline removed her shoes and tied the bottom of her dress around her upper legs. She walked in to where the water just came to her knees, opened the urn, and tossed her mother's ashes among the outgoing waves.

Cass watched as Faith stood for a few more minutes, head tilted up toward the sky, tears sliding down her cheeks as she said a silent good-bye to her mother. When Faith's shoulders began to shake, Cass walked out, not giving a second thought to her pants, and pulled Faith into her arms. Faith's arms wrapped tightly around Cass's waist as she buried her face along Cass's neck and wept for her loss.

They stood that way until the rising tide nudged them to go ashore. Cass kept her arm around Faith's waist as they trudged ashore and delivered her to the waiting arms of Nadine who smiled at Cass in gratitude as she gave Faith a motherly embrace and a peck on the forehead. As they walked back to their little camp, Faith grasped Cass's hand and held it tightly along the way. Upon their return, Faith walked back to the jeep then came back with a large envelope.

"Nadine and Serge, my mother left one final instruction." She handed the envelope to Nadine who opened it up, briefly looked it over, and gazed at Faith in confusion.

"What is this?" Nadine asked.

"Momma wanted you and Serge to have the property so that you can finally build your vacation inn. It's not only this lot but the two neighboring lots as well. Plenty of land to do everything you and Serge dreamed of doing. Instead of worrying about trying to save up to buy land and build out the property, now all you have to focus on is the build-out," Faith told her.

Serge took the papers from his mother's trembling hand and looked them over in the dim lantern lights in disbelief. "But what about the home you two were going to build here?" he asked.

"That was going to be Momma's retirement home. I didn't have any plans to do anything but visit, and I can do that at your inn."

Nadine rushed over and pulled Faith into a tight embrace. "I knew God blessed us when he brought you two into our lives all those years ago. Thank you."

Faith returned the hug. "No need to thank me. That was all Sabrina Shaw's doing."

Serge wiped away a tear and joined them for a group hug.

"Okay, enough tears! This is supposed to be a birthday celebration," Faith said.

She walked over to her phone, which was connected to the small speaker, pulled up the playlist she created of her mother's favorite dance music, pressed play, then began cutting the cake. Cass assisted by opening the sparkling cider and pouring glasses for everyone. They spent the next half hour laughing, dancing, and eating cake. Faith could not have imagined a better way to celebrate her mother's life. As they cleaned up, she looked at Serge and Nadine, her heart filled with love for her Caribbean family. When her gaze landed on Cass, she felt a tenderness she would not have expected so soon after meeting someone. The fact that Cass was cool with their first date ending with a memorial service for her mother showed a depth of compassion Faith was not used to seeing much of these days.

They said their good nights, and Faith and Cass headed back to the resort.

"Thank you," Faith said. "I know this isn't quite the date night you were expecting."

"Honestly, this is the best date I've had in a very long time."

"Really? Do you attend memorial services with all of your dates?"

Cass laughed. "This is a first for that. I was referring to my companion during the date."

Faith took Cass's hand. "I really am glad you were here. It felt right. Like our meeting was supposed to happen the way it did so that you could be here with me tonight."

Cass gave Faith's hand a gentle squeeze. "It does feel like we were destined to meet. First the train and then the beach this afternoon. I think I'm going to have to give my assistant a raise when I get back for sending me here."

Faith laughed and they drove back to the hotel, hands clasped just enjoying each other's presence. Arms around each other's waists, they walked through the lobby toward the direction of the villas stopping at the path that would take them in separate directions.

Faith turned fully toward Cass. "This has been an interesting day."

"Yes, it has. I wish it didn't have to end," Cass pulled Faith fully into her arms.

"It doesn't have to," Faith said with a sexy grin.

"Would you like to join me for a drink?"

"I was hoping you would ask," Faith said.

When they arrived at Cass's villa, there was a champagne bucket with a bottle of Faith's favorite wine and Cass's favorite beer on ice waiting for them.

"Serge is very good at his job."

"If not a bit presumptuous at times," Faith said in mock offense.

"Well, it saves us having to call room service," Cass said, opening the bottle of wine.

She handed a glass to Faith then grabbed one of the beers for herself. She grasped Faith's hand and led her over to the sofa. "Why don't you get comfortable?"

Faith removed her shoes, folded her legs beneath her, and sipped her wine. Cass sat beside her and fidgeted with her beer bottle, her heart rapidly beating in her chest and butterflies fluttering in her belly. She didn't know why she was suddenly so nervous, then she remembered when Ebony and Chayse had teased her about her "type" of woman. Looking at Faith, Cass realized that she was unlike any of the women she was used to dating. She had a tendency to go for vapid, materialistic women she didn't have to work too hard at impressing. Her name and money did the work for her. With Faith she knew it was different. Faith had no idea who she really was and was a successful woman in her own right so she wouldn't be the least impressed with what Cass could buy her.

Faith placed her wine glass on the coffee table, shifted closer to Cass, took the untouched beer out of her hands, placed it next to her wine glass, and then straddled Cass's lap.

"I've been wanting to do this since we kissed on the beach after dinner," she said before taking Cass's face into her hands and kissing her.

It didn't take much coaxing for Cass to slide her hands around Faith's waist to pull her in closer to deepen the kiss. Faith stroked Cass's back while Cass slid her hands along the curves of Faith's backside and gave a gentle but firm squeeze. Faith moaned into Cass's mouth and shifted her hips forward causing her most sensitive parts to come into contact with the fly of Cass's pants. Cass kissed along Faith's jawline to her neck, trailing a heated path toward her cleavage. When her tongue dipped out and traced the outline of Faith's breasts along the edge of her dress, she felt Faith's body tremble within her arms. Cass kissed her way back up toward Faith's ear.

"Should we stop?" she whispered.

"Why would we want to do that?" Faith asked breathlessly.

"I just wanted to make sure we aren't moving too fast."

Faith looked down to make eye contact with Cass. "Don't get me wrong, I don't normally do this on a first date, but I also don't normally feel such a strong pull toward someone on the first date either. Believe me when I say if I want this to stop, I will let you know. Besides, I believe I'm the one who started this," she said with a mischievous grin.

Cass slid her hands along Faith's thighs to where her dress bunched up around her knees and slid her hands beneath the hem before traveling back up and massaging the sensitive area of Faith's inner thighs with her thumbs. Faith's head fell back and a deep moan escaped at the intimate touch. Cass leaned forward and traced a warm trail of kisses along Faith's exposed neck as her fingers skimmed along the lace of her panties. Faith's whole body shivered in reaction.

"Are you cold?" Cass asked.

"Just the opposite."

Cass pressed the pad of her thumb against the area of Faith's panties where her clit was sheathed beneath, and she shivered once more. "Hmm...I wonder what could be causing such a reaction," she teased her.

Faith grasped Cass's face and brought her lips down upon hers in a passion-filled kiss as she shifted her hips closer to the pressure of Cass's thumb and rode the pleasure it brought to her clit until her panties were soaked with the proof of her desire.

Faith broke the kiss. "Why don't we take this to the bedroom."

Cass wrapped her arms tightly around Faith's waist, scooted forward on the sofa, and stood with Faith still in her arms. Faith wrapped her arms around Cass's neck and her legs around Cass's waist as she walked toward the bedroom. When they arrived, Cass gently lowered Faith onto the bed.

"Lie back," she told Faith, who didn't hesitate to comply.

Cass lifted the hem of Faith's dress, reached beneath to grasp her panties, and slowly pulled them down Faith's hips and along her long legs. Faith watched as Cass brought the lacy confection toward her nose, closed her eyes, and inhaled deeply.

Cass tossed the panties aside and knelt between Faith's legs. "Let's find out if you taste as good as you smell."

Faith spread her legs wider to accommodate Cass who bunched the hem of her dress farther up around her hips and lowered her head between Faith's smooth thighs. Cass lowered her head and placed her lips for the most intimate of kisses. Faith whimpered in response. When Cass lifted Faith's legs and placed them on her shoulders and her tongue slowly snaked out and flicked her clit, it took Faith everything she had to keep from flying off the bed. She gripped the bedding to hold herself down as Cass proceeded to give her a tongue lashing she would never forget.

Faith's whimpers soon turned to moans, then to Cass's surprise, passionate murmurs in French. Cass held on to Faith's hips and rode out the tide of shudders and squirming until she felt Faith's body stiffen just before she shouted out in orgasmic release. Cass plunged her tongue deep as the proof of Faith's climax pooled from the heart of her femininity. As the aftershocks of Faith's pleasure tremored through her body, Cass joined her on the bed lying beside her. Cass rested her head on her hand and lazily ran her fingers up and down Faith's thigh.

"So you speak French?" Cass asked.

"Uh, yeah, how did you know?"

Cass repeated some of what Faith said and Faith covered her face in embarrassment.

"Judging by your expression I guess I'm going to have to google it to find out what you said."

Faith peeked out between her fingers, "Maybe I'll tell you at breakfast."

"Breakfast. Does that mean I get another French lesson?" Cass said as her index finger slipped into the slick opening of Faith's sex and stroked lazily.

Faith moaned. "Mm-hm." was her only response.

Cass leaned over and covered Faith's mouth with her own, her tongue exploring the same way her fingers were exploring within Faith's other lips. Faith's hips moved in response. But before she could bring Faith to another orgasm, Cass stopped her ministrations.

Cass felt a sense of satisfaction at Faith's whimper of frustration at being stopped so close to completion. "Let's get out of these clothes. I want to see all of you," she told her.

Faith stood and, before Cass could even remove her own shirt, she quickly removed her dress and bra. Cass's breath caught at the sight of Faith standing before her in all her naked glory. She dropped her shirt on the floor and walked over to Faith.

"You are so beautiful," Cass said. She rested her hands on Faith's waist, bent her head, and took one of Faith's hardened nipples into her mouth, gently suckling and nibbling until Faith was moaning once again.

Faith ran her hands along Cass's scalp and thrust her chest forward. Cass took her other hand and began massaging Faith's other breast while she suckled on the first.

"Not fair…" Faith said breathlessly. "You're still dressed."

"What do you know, I sure am." She stepped back and finished undressing.

Faith ran her fingers lightly over Cass's abs. She knelt in front of Cass and replaced her fingers with her tongue, tracing the outline of every muscle as her hands massaged along Cass's hips and buttocks. Cass moaned and buried her fingers in Faith's hair. When Faith's tongue trailed its way down Cass's hip bone toward the juncture of her thighs Cass's legs almost buckled beneath her.

"Let's try the bed," she gently grasped Faith's shoulders to encourage her to stand.

Faith walked the short distance to the bed and lay down. Cass joined her, settling her body over Faith's. Cass kissed her hungrily, as if she couldn't get enough of the feel and taste of Faith's lips.

Faith playfully nudged Cass off of her. "My turn."

Cass lay back and casually clasped her hands behind her head. "Do as you will."

"Turn over," Faith commanded.

Cass hesitated but did as she was told. She felt Faith leave the bed and heard her padding away. She was back a moment later and climbed back on the bed.

"Relax," Faith told her.

Cass tried to look back over her shoulder at Faith. "What are you going to do?" she asked nervously.

Faith leaned down and placed a kiss on Cass's frown. "You really don't like not being in control, do you? Just relax, I'm not going to do anything you won't enjoy."

Cass crossed her arms and laid her head down trying to relax. She heard the pop of a top, then a few seconds later, smelled the scent of her favorite lotion and felt Faith's soft hands spreading the thick cream along her shoulders.

"Wow, you are beyond tense. It's like trying to massage a concrete wall," Faith said, firmly kneading Cass's tight shoulders.

Cass took a deep breath and allowed herself to relax under Faith's attentive ministrations. Her hands and fingers were strong and were soon coaxing the tension from Cass's neck, shoulders, and back. Listening to the faint sound of the ocean beyond the open window, feeling Faith's firm touch, and having no current care in the world except this moment had Cass wondering if this was what Heaven felt like.

Faith was thoroughly enjoying turning the controlling, tense woman she'd met this afternoon to butter. She had her turn over onto her back and repeated the same massaging touch along the front of her body. She took extra time to gently knead her breasts, purposely bypassing the sensitive area at the juncture of her thighs and working her way to Cass's feet where she found out Cass was ticklish when she began giggling as Faith tried to massage her feet.

"Ah, I've found a weakness," Faith teased her.

"And I hope you keep it to yourself."

"What happens in Turks and Caicos stays in Turks and Caicos," Faith joked.

Cass gently pulled Faith on top of her. "I hope not everything," she said sincerely.

"Not if I can help it." Faith cupped Cass's face and placed a gentle, sweet kiss on her lips.

The next few hours were spent making slow, passionate love until both were too satiated to do anything but fall asleep in each other's arms.

❖

Cass awoke to the sound of light snoring. She opened her eyes and smiled as her gaze landed on the woman sleeping beside her making the noise. She couldn't believe how the past twenty-four hours had completely changed her. Since the moment she'd met Faith on the beach she had not once thought about what might be going on at Pure. For the first time in years, she was actually enjoying just being with someone without wondering how she was going to get the woman out of her house before she had to get up and start her day. She felt as if she could simply lie there watching Faith sleep all morning. She almost laughed at a particularly loud snort

Faith's eyes fluttered opened. "Are you really watching me sleep?"

"More like watching you snore," Cass said with an amused grin.

Faith covered her head with the sheet. "I can't believe I just did that." She peeked out at Cass.

"I've discovered your weakness. Now we're even." She moved the sheet from in front of Faith's face and greeted her with a deep kiss.

"Good morning, beautiful," Cass said.

"Good morning, sexy," Faith responded.

"You hungry?" Cass asked.

"Starved."

"Serge stocks the fridge in case I want anything while he's not available. Let me see what I can throw together." Cass placed a quick kiss on Faith's nose then climbed out of bed.

Faith watched admiringly as Cass quickly dressed in her T-shirt and boxer briefs from last night then left the room in search of food. She fell back happily into the covers and stretched lazily. Meeting Cass was such a wonderfully unexpected treat from what she thought was going to be a sad trip. Cass had mentioned interest in looking at property on the island, and Faith thought it would be a great way to spend the day. She would contact the Realtor who helped her mother find her property and see what was available to view that afternoon. Faith smiled to herself. Funny how life works. A chance encounter on a train leading to this wonderful moment.

The sound of buzzing interrupted her thoughts. She looked over at the nightstand and saw that it was Cass's phone. She was just about to let Cass know when she noticed the picture of the person and name that came up with the call. The caller ID said Chanelle, and the picture was one of Cass and Chanelle Lawson, heads together, smiling happily at the camera in a selfie pic. Faith sat up staring at the phone as if Chanelle herself were about to appear in the room with her.

When the buzzing stopped, sending the call to voice mail, Faith sat staring at it in confusion.

How did Chanelle and Cass know each other? Then she remembered something Cass told her when they were talking about their families. She had an uncle who was the black sheep of the family and had involved his kids in his schemes. What were the chances that Cass's uncle was Craig Lawson? What were the chances that the chance meeting on the beach wasn't a chance meeting at all but something Craig had arranged to try to compromise her or to get her to sell the house?

Faith's mind swirled with confusion and doubt. Even if it wasn't planned, and the encounter on the train then meeting here was a coincidence, there was no way she was going to get involved with anyone connected to Craig Lawson. Faith jumped out of bed, hurriedly dressed, searched the room for her shoes, then remembered she'd left them in the living room. She would have to leave them. Fortunately, sometime during the night she had brought her phone into the room with her ID, credit cards, and room key stored in the stick-on wallet. She grabbed her phone and left through the door that led out to the same patio that the living room doors faced. She made sure to walk around the villa in the opposite direction of where those doors faced so Cass wouldn't see her. Tears clouded her vision as she ran barefoot all the way to her villa.

❖

"Here we go!" Cass said as she walked into the bedroom with a tray of sliced fruit, toast, a veggie omelet, and mimosas.

She stopped on the threshold when she noticed the empty bed. "Faith?" she called.

When there was no answer, she placed the tray on the desk in the room and walked toward the open bathroom door.

"Faith?" When she saw the bathroom was empty, she looked around the room in confusion. Then she noticed the open patio door.

"You want to have breakfast on the patio?" she asked as she grabbed the tray again and walked over to the door. Once again, confusion reigned when she didn't find Faith outside.

She set the tray on one of the patio tables and walked out to the beach, then around the perimeter of the villa but didn't find Faith. When she started getting strange looks from passersby, she realized she was walking around in her underwear and hurried back into the villa. She put on her pants, slipped on her shoes, grabbed her phone, then headed back out to the living room with the intention of going to Faith's villa, then she realized she didn't know which one was hers. They had spent most of their time together at her villa. Cass sat on the sofa, head in hands, trying to figure out what she might have said or done to make Faith leave so abruptly, but she couldn't think of anything.

She was still sitting that way when there was a knock on her door. Cass hurried to answer it.

"Faith, I thought you—" But it wasn't Faith on the other side of the door. It was Serge.

"Good morning, Cass. I figured after your late night you would want to sleep in today so I thought you wouldn't mind if I came a little late," he said.

"Oh, hey, Serge." She walked dejectedly away from the door, leaving it open for him to enter.

Serge looked on in concern. "Is everything all right?" he asked.

"I honestly don't know," she said.

Before she could explain further, her phone buzzed in her pocket. She pulled it out and saw Ebony's name.

"Yo, Eb, what's up?" she asked.

"Hey, Cass, sorry to interrupt your vacay, but we have an issue and unfortunately you're the only one that can handle it. How soon can you get to the airport?"

Cass ran her hand tiredly down her face. "Give me an hour."

"Okay. Steph already called to have the plane ready for whenever you get there. Call me when you get to the airport and I'll give you more details."

"Yeah, okay," Cass said then hung up.

"Serge, I have to leave." Cass felt a migraine coming on.

"No worries. I'll have you all packed and a car waiting to take you to the airport by the time you finish your shower," he promised, still watching her worriedly.

"Thanks." Cass headed into the bedroom. On her way, she noticed something red peeking out from beneath the coffee table. She walked over to find Faith had left her shoes behind. Cass picked them up and stared down at them in disbelief. Once again, she racked her brain wondering what could have happened that she would be in such a rush that she didn't even bother grabbing her shoes or saying good-bye?

With a sigh, she carried the shoes into the bedroom, stuffed them into her backpack, grabbed a pair of clean undergarments, jeans, and a T-shirt on her way to the bathroom, and was ready within forty-five minutes.

Serge waited by the front door with her bag. "There's a car waiting at the hotel for you. It's been a pleasure attending to you, Cass."

"Thank you, Serge. You've been great and I'll make sure the head honchos know it," she said with a small smile.

"You sure there is nothing else I can do for you before you go?" he asked.

Cass hesitated. "If you see Faith..." She wasn't even sure what she could say to her. She shook her head. "Never mind. Thanks again for everything, Serge. Good luck to you and your mom with the inn." She pulled out one of her business cards and handed it to him. "Be sure to let me know when you're up and running. I'd like to be one of your first guests."

Serge looked down at the card, and his eyes widened in surprise at Cass's title. "I will definitely do that."

They shook hands and Cass walked out feeling as if her whole world had just collapsed beneath her feet.

Faith sat at her drafting table staring at a blank piece of paper. She was supposed to be drafting up various ideas for a custom order, but her heart just wasn't in it. She had been back from Turks and Caicos for a week now, and she just couldn't get Cass and how she had left things with her off of her mind.

She realized a couple of hours after she had run out that she should have given Cass an opportunity to explain. After all, she did say she and the family didn't really talk to her uncle that often so there was no way she would have been involved in any schemes Craig had going. She had also realized that the sister who called her mother and told her the truth about Craig was more than likely Cass's mother.

Unfortunately, by the time she swallowed her pride and walked back over to Cass's villa, she had left. Serge was there with housekeeping prepping the villa for a new guest and told her Cass had an emergency and had left that morning. When Serge told her how upset Cass seemed Faith almost cried and poured her heart out to Serge. He told her what she already knew; she had been foolish to leave the way she did. Not seeing any reason to prolong her stay any longer, Faith had booked a flight out the next day. She couldn't even call Cass and apologize because she had never gotten a chance to get her phone number. Even though Cass had her business card, Faith doubted she would be calling her after what she had done.

A knock on her door interrupted her thoughts. She looked up to find Ezra standing in the doorway.

"Hey, beautiful," he said in his usual greeting.

Faith met him halfway across the room. He gave her one of his healing bear hugs and a kiss on the cheek.

"You always seem to know when I need one of your hugs," she said.

"Uh-oh, what's going on?" he asked, looking at her in concern.

"Foolish pride stuff," she said.

"Anything I can do besides supply hugs?" he asked.

"Not really," she indicated they should sit on the sofa in her office. "What brings you to my humble shop?"

"Well, Craig Lawson is dropping the claim on the house, and they have vacated the property," Ezra told her.

"Good riddance," Faith said in relief.

"Unfortunately, not quite. It seems he made a couple of shady real estate deals and forged your mother's signature on them, and now the contractors have come to collect since they can't seem to find him."

Faith buried her face in her hands. "He's like a bad penny that just keeps showing up. What's the damage?"

Ezra hesitated in answering.

Faith looked at him worriedly. "Ezra."

"Ten thousand dollars."

"You're kidding," Faith shouted.

"You know I would not kid about something like this, especially concerning that crook."

Faith walked over to a window "What are our options?"

"They're threatening to sue if we don't pay what's owed. I think we can fight it, but it may take some time since Craig has conveniently dropped off the face of the earth," he said.

"For now, until his next victim," Faith said angrily. "Pay them."

"Are you sure? I think we should fight it out. That's a lot of money to just give away."

"Craig Lawson has caused enough trouble. I just want it over with and him out of my life," Faith said tiredly.

"Okay. Let me see if I can get that number down considering this all occurred while your mother was in hospice at the time the deals happened and there was no way she was in the frame of mind to make deals."

"Thank you, Ezra."

"The other reason I'm here is to ask if you would like to be my plus one for a charity event coming up."

"I don't feel much like partying, Ezra. Besides, wouldn't you want to go with a real date? Someone you have a chance at a romantic connection with?"

"Honestly, there's no one I'm interested in asking, and I think it will do you some good to get out and socialize. There could also be a business opportunity for you. I got a tip from a client that one of the suppliers included in the swag bags they are giving to the platinum donors pulled out and they're looking for swag from an upcoming fashionista to replace her."

Faith turned toward him, "Seriously?"

"Seriously. I was thinking you can offer your custom shoe designs. Just imagine some big name celebrities strutting the red carpets in a custom pair of Glass Slippers," Ezra said.

Faith's mind raced with the possibilities this opportunity could afford her.

"So, what's it gonna be? Sitting at home on another Friday night or schmoozing with some of the biggest names in the entertainment industry?" Ezra asked with a knowing grin.

"Who do I need to talk to?" Faith said.

"Now that's the Faith I know." He pulled a card from his wallet and handed it to her. "Her name is Eve Monroe. She's the event planner. I told her to expect your call."

Faith took the card. "And what if I had said no?"

"I know you better than that. I'll call you soon about the contractors."

They embraced once more. "Thank you, Ezra. You're a good friend," Faith said sincerely.

"Who are you kidding, I'm your only friend," he said with a wink, chuckling as he ran out of the room before the pencil Faith threw at him could hit its mark.

❖

"Not the fashion choice I picture you in, but hey, who am I to judge," Ebony said as she walked into Cass's office. Cass was staring at Faith's red stiletto shoes on her desk.

Cass laughed. "They're not quite my size." She placed the shoes on the credenza behind her. "What's up, Eb?"

"I just want to go over the final run-through for tonight. I ran into Steph heading out to meet Eve for the setup, and she said you had a couple of questions."

They discussed the guest list, performers, song lists, and the meet and greet scheduled with the performers and media after the event.

"Also, we sold out of the one hundred tickets we offered to the public," Ebony told her.

"Great. So we're all set then," Cass said.

"Yeah. What about you? Are you all set?" Ebony asked.

"What do you mean? I'm good."

"C'mon, Cass, ever since you got back from Turks and Caicos you've been in some kind of funk. You keep saying you aren't mad at us, but something is bothering you. And what's up with the shoes?"

Cass sat back in her chair and told Ebony about what happened with her and Faith. When she was finished she felt as if a huge cloud had cleared from her mind and she was able to think clearly.

"Wow," Ebony said. "And you haven't tried to contact her since you got back?"

Cass shrugged. "Why? She obviously didn't want to continue what we started after returning to New York or why else would she have left the way she did. Maybe I was just a pleasant distraction from having to deal with the loss of her mother."

"So you think she just meant for you to be a one-night stand?" Ebony asked.

"I don't know. She obviously wanted to get out of there so fast she slipped out the back door without her shoes," Cass pointed to the red shoes on the credenza behind her.

"Those are hers? You actually brought them back? Why if you hadn't planned on contacting her? You could have easily given them to the butler to return since they're friends," Ebony said.

Cass grabbed one of the shoes, balancing the heel in the palm of her hand. "I don't know. I guess I just wanted something to remember the time with."

"What if you could talk to her and ask why?" Ebony asked.

"Don't see how that will happen unless I call her, which I don't plan on doing."

Ebony opened her iPad and scrolled through something on the screen. When she was finished, she laid the screen in front of Cass. "This is the list for the swag bag vendors. Scroll down to the bottom."

Cass did as Ebony said, her eyes widening as she saw the last vendor on the list. She looked up at Ebony suspiciously. "When did this happen and how long have you known?"

"Stephanie sent me the list this morning. Said Essential Fashions had to pull their swag item out due to some issues with the product. Eve had mentioned something to her attorney who is attending the ball, and he told her about one of his other clients who might be interested in adding her product. Everything was handled by Eve and Stephanie a couple of weeks ago and I just found out this morning," Ebony explained.

Cass looked back down at the name on the list and felt her heart skip a beat. "Does she know who the event is for?"

Ebony shrugged. "I'm assuming she does since she spoke with Stephanie. So what are you going to do?"

Cass looked at the shoe sitting beside the iPad and smiled. "I need you to do me a favor."

❖

Faith paced nervously in front of her bedroom mirror. "I don't know what I was thinking agreeing to do this."

Ezra watched her in confusion. "Faith, it's just a charity ball and your costume looks fantastic. What are you so anxious about?"

Faith stopped and gazed at her reflection in the mirror. The event theme was an enchanted garden masquerade ball. Faith had created a fairy costume to go along with Ezra's elf. She wore a flowy sparkling gown with a halter top and a flowy skirt that gave the impression of dozens of gossamer scarves stitched together so when she walked each layer flowed as if she were caught in a constant breeze. Her shoes resembled open toe glass slippers with a stiletto heel and silk ribbons that laced up to her knee. The finishing touch was a set of gossamer fairy wings she had also created herself. She used colored hair spray to give her hair a gold hue and her makeup consisted of glittery gold shadows, stick-on jewels, and dramatic eyelashes. She had to admit she did look fantastic, but she didn't feel it.

As soon as she had contacted Eve Monroe and found out Pure Music was hosting the charity ball she was committing to, she had seriously considered changing her mind. There was no doubt she would run into Cass at the event, she just had to figure out how to avoid any prolonged face time with her. After all this time she was too embarrassed to bother trying to explain why she ran out the way she did and hadn't even tried to contact Cass when she returned.

Serge told her Cass took her shoes so she had hoped she would be the one to reach out, but when Faith didn't hear from her she knew she had screwed up too badly to fix anything. For all she knew, Cass could have given her shoes to some other woman. After all, they were from one of her best designs and practically brand new. Faith had only worn them twice and that included the night with Cass. Faith flopped dejectedly down beside Ezra.

"Faith, what the hell is going on with you?"

"There's something I should warn you about before we go to this event."

Faith told Ezra everything about Cass from the subway encounter to when she ran out on her in Turks and Caicos. Ezra sat and listened quietly, then when Faith finished he looked at her curiously for a moment.

"Would you say something?" she said in annoyance.

"You really don't know who Cass is, do you?" he said.

"I told you. She said she's a producer at Pure Music. Why are you grinning like a Cheshire cat?"

"Faith, I simply adore you, but you really should read something more than sales reports and fashion industry literature. First of all, Cass Phillips is not just a producer for Pure Music, she is the CEO and owner."

Faith looked at Ezra in confusion. "We must be talking about two different people. She told me she was just a producer."

Ezra pulled out his phone and pulled up an article from *XXL* magazine about Cass with her picture plastered right at the top standing casually in front of a trophy case filled with various music industry awards.

"Why wouldn't she tell me who she really is?"

"A successful woman like that with the money she has, there are gold diggers left and right trying to get at her. Can you blame her for not saying anything to some woman she'd just met on the beach. Then you didn't even bother sticking around knowing she was just a producer. If she had told you the truth and you had stayed she really wouldn't know if you had done it because you genuinely liked her or her bank account," Ezra said.

"But I'm not like that," Faith said angrily.

"How was she to know that? You guys literally met and slept together all within a twenty-four-hour period and then you dashed before you could even take the time to really get to know each other. How would that look to you?"

Faith sat quietly for a moment and thought about what happened, then sighed. "I was the one who asked her to lunch and dinner. I was the one who pretty much threw myself into her bed, and it now looks like I'm the one who ghosted her."

"Exactly. Would you contact someone that did that to you?" Ezra asked in that reasonable lawyer tone of his. She always hated when he was right.

"That doesn't explain how she knows Chanelle," Faith said, not wanting to fully admit blame for the situation.

"If you had stuck around to ask you would have found out, but since you didn't I can fill you in on that," Ezra said matter-of-factly.

Faith looked at him in confusion again.

"When your mother got the call from Craig's sister, she asked me to look further into him and his family. His sister is Cass's mother, but she had not been involved with her brother for several years because he had run one of his real estate scams on her and her husband and almost bankrupted them. Cass has talked about this in early bios about her life. She had been trying to help her cousin Chanelle with her music career at the time, and they had a falling out when Cass found out Chanelle knew about the scam the whole time and didn't say anything.

Cass ended up bailing her parents out of the situation, but she refused to continue helping Chanelle. The Lawsons have been outcasts from the family ever since. I couldn't imagine why she would have been calling Cass, but it wasn't because Cass knew what they were doing."

Faith laid her head back on the sofa and groaned painfully. "I can't believe I screwed this up so badly."

Ezra stood, grasped Faith's hands, and pulled her up with him. "Well, here's your opportunity to fix it and possibly win the heart of a wealthy businesswoman."

Faith smiled affectionately at Ezra. "What would I do without you?"

Ezra shrugged. "Probably spend the rest of your life single and clueless," he said, then placed an affectionate kiss on her cheek. "Now, put your wings on and let's go capture us a CEO."

Cass walked into the Chelsea Market Passage on the High Line and felt as if she had just stepped into a real life enchanted forest. Moss and ivy dripped from above and along the walls intermingled with fairy lights and paper lanterns. Imitation grass covered all but the center of the space where room was left clear for dancing. The performance stage stood amongst a copse of faux flowering trees. The sound of birds chirping mingled with a live harpist and violinist playing in the background setting the enchanted mood. They had also obtained usage of the High Line Sundeck which connected to the Chelsea Market Passage to accommodate the overflow of guests. The deck's natural greenery and view of the Hudson was all the décor needed so they simply added heat lamps along the deck.

"What do you think?" Stephanie asked.

"It looks unbelievable. Eve is a miracle worker," Cass said.

"It is fabulous. If you'd like to thank her, she and Lynette are in the catering tent with Chayse and her crew."

"Great, I'll go find them in a bit. Right now I want to thank you for all of your hard work." Cass handed Stephanie an envelope.

Stephanie took the envelope. "What's this?" She asked.

"Ebony and I just want to show you our appreciation for all of your hard work. You're so busy taking care of everyone else we don't want you to forget to take care of yourself as well."

Stephanie opened the envelope and found confirmation for an all-expense paid one-week vacation for the very resort they had sent Cass to.

Stephanie smiled with tears in her eyes and pulled Cass into a tight hug. "Thank you. I was so jealous planning your vacation," she admitted.

"Well, you can enjoy it now except no one will be calling you to fly back for artist temper tantrums."

Stephanie smiled guiltily. "Thank you again. Now I have to go fix my makeup." She wiped away a stray tear.

Laughing, Cass watched her walk away then headed to the catering tent where she found Chayse reprimanding Ebony for stealing food. Cass smiled as she watched her two best friends bickering and their better halves laughing at their antics. She greeted Belinda and Serena with hugs and kisses and Chayse and Ebony with hearty slaps on the back.

"Ebony, you keep eating like that you're gonna bust out of that tux before the end of the night," Cass teased her.

Chayse picked up a butcher knife and waved it in mock threat. "She keeps it up she's going to draw back nubs for fingers."

Ebony raised her hands in surrender. "Hey, I was just taste testing. Gotta make sure our guests are getting good food."

"All right, don't let me have to separate you two. Eb, is everything with that favor I asked for taken care of?" Cass asked Ebony.

"Yep, everything is set for right after Cree's performance."

Eve joined them greeting Cass with a hug.

"Eve, you did a fantastic job. It's exactly the vision I had and you brought it to life," Cass said, followed by applause from everyone around them.

Eve blushed. "Thank you, now we just have to get through the rest of the night."

"I'm sure with you, Chayse, and Stephanie running the show it'll be great. Ebony told you what I had planned?"

"Yes, and I think it's wonderful and you look very much the part."

"Let's just hope someone else feels the same way," Cass said.

"What are you supposed to be anyway?" Chayse asked, indicating Cass's outfit.

"Can't you tell? Prince Charming," Cass did a fashionable turn.

"And who is the princess our Prince Charming is trying to capture?" Serena asked.

"She's more of a Cinderella than a princess," Belinda said.

Cass frowned at Ebony. "You told her?"

"Bro, I tell her everything, you ought to know that by now," Ebony said.

Serena looked at Chayse expectantly.

Chayse shrugged. "Hey, I don't know anything. I'm just here to cook."

Belinda clasped Serena's hand. "C'mon, I'll tell you while we grab a glass of champagne."

Cass watched them. "Those two becoming friends was trouble from the start."

Ebony laughed and placed an affectionate hand on Cass's shoulder. "They have the right idea. Let's get you a drink. You need to loosen up."

They said their farewells for now to Chayse and Eve and headed back to the main event area.

Ezra exited their car first and reached back to assist Faith. The event's scheduled start time was just a half hour ago, but there was already a line of people waiting to be checked in.

"Wow." Faith recognized some celebrity faces in spite of their costumes as they made their way to the end of the line. "This really is a star-studded event."

"I told you. Aren't you glad I talked you into it and that Stephanie insisted you provide Frenetic and Cree with their shoes for tonight?"

Faith had been working with Eve and Stephanie, an assistant from Pure Music, and had been hesitant when Stephanie suggested having their new artists wear her shoes because she thought she would be the best model for her own product. Then Stephanie reminded her that the artists would be on stage for everyone to see, what better advertisement. She had met with both artists to find out what their costumes were going to be for the night and customized their footwear to match. Cree planned to dress as a dark fairy so Faith designed a pair of black peep toe rhinestone stiletto ankle boots and Frenetic refused to wear a costume but wanted a pair of leopard print shoes to go with his black leather suit so that's what Faith gave him. They weren't the most original design, but they were well made.

The line moved quickly in spite of the paparazzi crowding the sidewalk. When they walked into the venue space, Faith was thoroughly impressed. It was like walking into another world. A server dressed in a sexy fox costume greeted them at the entrance.

"Welcome to the enchanted garden. May I offer you a cup of ambrosia?" she asked.

Ezra took two glasses of the purple concoction she offered. "Thank you," he said, then handed one to Faith. "To a successful night in business and the heart." He tapped his glass to Faith's in a toast.

Faith took a sip of the drink. "Whoa, that is strong."

"Ambrosia is the drink of the gods, it's supposed to be strong." Ezra took a longer sip if his drink.

Faith chuckled. "Slow down now. I need you to stay sober as long as possible to get me through this night."

"My momma's rum punch would put this stuff to shame, and I've been drinking that since I was sixteen so I'll be good." He looped her arm in his as they strolled through the growing crowd.

As they walked around, Faith realized that her costume wasn't as original as she thought it would be. There were various versions of fairies floating around the room, some with much more outlandish outfits than hers. Eve had asked what she would be wearing so she could be sure to have Stephanie grab her when they introduced the swag bag suppliers. Since they had never met in person, there was no way they were going to be able to tell which fairy was her.

Cass stood at the edge of the stage peering around one of the trees looking over the crowd arriving. Eve told her Faith was going to be dressed as a fairy, but she should have known better than to think she would be easy to pick out amongst a crowd at an enchanted garden costume party. She had never seen so many fairies in her life.

"How's it going?" Ebony asked, peeking around her.

"Not good. Was there an oversupply of fairy wings somewhere? It seems like every woman in the place is a fairy," Cass said in frustration.

Ebony laughed.

Cass gazed back at her annoyed. "What's so funny?"

"I'm just imagining every fairy in the room lining up to try on the shoe. Just like the real Cinderella story."

Cass tried and failed not to also laugh at the image of how badly that would go.

"Why don't we divide and conquer. You and Stephanie actually know what she looks like, and I'm sure Serena, Eve, and I can google a pic of her, then we can all walk the crowd to see if we can spot her," Ebony offered.

Cass sighed in resignation. "That sounds like a good idea."

An hour later, Cass stood backstage feeling frustrated. There were just too many people, and she had to MC the show so her plans for Faith would have to wait. She stepped out onto the stage to welcome everyone and introduce the first performer then stepped back into the wings and tried once again to look over the crowd, but she couldn't see much farther than the stage due to the spotlights.

❖

Faith's heart skipped a beat when Cass stepped out onto the stage. She drank in everything about her appearance as she spoke, not even hearing a word she was saying. She looked so hot dressed in black leather pants that emphasized her rounded tight behind, a sleeveless fitted silver and black tapestry military style waistcoat that showed off her muscular arms, and a black metal crown with jeweled rhinestones. It was as if she were trying to look like…

"Is it me or does she look like she's a prince for the night?" Ezra asked as if reading Faith's thoughts.

Ezra turned toward Faith. "Prince Charming, mystery woman, and a lost shoe, does any of this sound familiar to you?" he said with a grin.

"What?" Faith asked unconvincingly as if she didn't know what he was getting at.

"Cinderella. She knew you would be here and probably has your shoes waiting on a silk pillow in the wings until she finds you to slip it onto your foot."

"I seriously doubt that," Faith said.

"Where's your imagination and sense of romance?"

"When did you become such a romantic?"

"Since I realized my best friend is finally in love," he said with a grin.

"In love? I can't be. I barely know her." Faith watched longingly as Cass left the stage.

"Yeah, okay. Come dance with me." He pulled her toward the dance floor as the first performance of the night began.

There were about a dozen other couples on the dance floor. Faith allowed herself to relax and let the music carry her away. She loved dancing and Ezra had always been a great partner because he loved it as much as she did. As they danced, the floor became more crowded, and before Faith realized what was happening she was being pulled away from Ezra. The crowd soon separated them, and she looked to see who had grabbed her arm. A man in a phantom of the opera mask was pulling her along. She attempted to yank her arm away, but his grip was too tight.

"Let me go!" she shouted to no avail.

The music was too loud and no one was paying them any mind as she was dragged along.

They ended up on the sundeck of the High Line where it was less crowded. The man finally released her, and she stepped back to avoid being grabbed again.

"Who the hell do you think you are?" she asked angrily.

She was shocked as he removed his mask.

"Craig? What are doing here? Are you following me?"

"I'm just as surprised to see you here," he said, not answering her question.

Faith turned to walk away but was blocked by another woman dressed as a fairy. It didn't take her long to recognize Monet, Craig's oldest daughter.

Monet sneered at her. "Look at this, we get to hit two birds with one stone."

"What are you both doing here?" Faith asked.

"We came here to talk to my cousin Cass and happened to spot you in the crowd. I suggested we have a little chat with you before we speak to Cass. You owe us," Monet said angrily.

"Owe you? For what? You're lucky I don't have you all locked up for what you tried to do to my mother. What you're trying to do to me. I don't owe you a damn thing!" Faith moved to walk past Monet who reached out her birdlike talons and grabbed Faith's arm.

Monet yanked her back and put her face so close to Faith's she was practically kissing her. "You bitch! You think you're better than us, you always have. My father did more for your mother than he ever did for any woman and you treat him like a common thief."

"That's because that's what he is. In spite of everything, in spite of what my mother learned about him, she still took care of him. Still left him more than enough money and assets for the three of you to live off for quite some time yet you're too greedy to see how lucky you are," Faith twisted her arm in a move she learned in her self-defense class to release Monet's grasp and backed away.

"If either one of you touch me again I will hurt you," she said, taking a defensive stance. She didn't know how much she could do in stiletto heels, but she wasn't going down without a fight.

Monet took a step toward her, and Faith raised her hand to strike.

"Monet!"

Both Faith and Monet turned toward the sound of her name being called. To Faith's relief, Cass, Ezra, and two security guards were walking toward them.

"What the hell is going on here?" Cass asked, looking angrily from Monet to Craig.

"Are you all right?" Ezra asked Faith.

"I'm fine," she said

Craig stepped forward. "Cass, Chanelle has been trying to reach you, but you haven't been returning her calls."

"Yeah, that's on purpose. The only time one of you reaches out to me is for money. I'm done bailing you all out of whatever schemes you have going," Cass said angrily.

"Cass, we're family. We're supposed to be there for each other in time of need. If I don't get ten thousand dollars to some people they're going to hurt me," Craig whined.

"How did you all get into the party?" she asked.

"We had to buy tickets like some common nobody." Monet looked at her father in disgust. "Daddy, we didn't come here to beg these people for shit. Let's go."

"Monet, shut up!" Craig shouted. "We're in this situation because you act like money grows on trees. Spending thousands of dollars on clothes, half of which you don't even wear. Now let me handle this!" He turned back to Cass.

"Look, Cass, I know I did your mom wrong, but this is serious. You know I wouldn't come to you if it wasn't. I owe some bad people money and they are coming to collect. If you won't do it for me, then at least do it for Chanelle. She never asked for or took a thing from anyone. I'm begging you, niece, please," Craig said pitifully.

Cass looked at Monet and Craig. "Chanelle might not have done anything directly, but she was complicit in everything you all did which makes her just as guilty. No, Uncle Craig, I'm not helping you, and if I ever see any of you anywhere within my vicinity, I will have you arrested. Now get out." Cass signaled for the two security men to escort them out.

If looks could kill, Faith and Cass would have died a painful death by the look Monet gave them as they were manhandled out the party.

Cass walked over to Faith and cupped her face in her hands. "Are you all right? Did they hurt you?" she asked.

"No, I'm fine. Just a little shaken. How did you know what was going on?"

Cass turned to Ezra. "Ezra had one of the security personnel find me and let me know what was happening. How do you know my uncle and cousin?"

"Remember the con artist my mother married?" Faith said.

Cass shook her head. "My uncle."

"Yeah."

"I'm sorry," Cass said.

"For what? You had nothing to do with what they did. As the old saying goes, you can pick your nose, but you can't pick your family," Faith said with a grin.

Cass laughed. "I missed you." She grasped Faith's hands.

Ezra cleared his throat. "Faith, you're in good hands. I'm just going to go get a drink. I'll catch up with you in a bit."

"Okay. Thank you, Ez."

Cass led Faith over to a nearby lounge chair.

"Faith, what happened in Turks and Caicos? Why did you leave?" Cass asked.

Faith looked down in embarrassment. "While you were fixing us breakfast, your phone rang. I happened to look over and saw the pic of you and Chanelle come up and her name on the caller ID. I couldn't imagine how you would know her and remembered you telling me about your uncle and cousins. I stupidly jumped to the conclusion that us meeting wasn't by chance and that maybe you were helping them get to me."

"Wow," Cass said.

"I know I should have probably just stuck around and asked, but having just said good-bye to my mom my emotions were still very raw. When I finally did realize my mistake and went back to talk to you, Serge told me you'd left." Faith felt too guilty to meet Cass's eyes.

Cass gently grasped Faith's chin and raised her head so she could look into her eyes. "I think we both made mistakes that day. I should have called you once I got back to find out what happened."

"I'm sorry." Faith took Cass's hand in hers.

"I'm sorry too. For what you went through with the loss of your mother and what my relatives put you through. But I am not sorry for what happened before the misunderstanding. Faith, I have never felt about any woman the way I feel about you. From the moment I saw you on that train you had my heart." Cass brought Faith's hands to her lips and pressed a kiss to her knuckles.

"Ezra thinks I'm in love with you," Faith said with smile.

"And what do you think?"

Faith released Cass's hands and cupped her face. "As impossible as it seems, I think he might be right." She brought Cass's face toward hers for a kiss that was so sweet and gentle it made Cass's heart skip a beat.

When their kiss ended, Cass stood and pulled Faith up along with her. "Come with me. I have to take care of a few things, but afterward I have a surprise for you."

When they finally reached their destination, which turned out to be backstage, Cree was finishing up her performance.

"There you are," Ebony said. "I didn't think you were going to make it."

"I got sidetracked," Cass said.

"Yeah, security informed me what happened," Ebony said then turned to Faith.

"Hey, I'm Ebony. I'm assuming you're the woman who's got Cass all twisted." She held a hand out in greeting to Faith.

Faith stared in surprise for a moment then took her hand. "Uh, yes, and nice to meet you. I'm a big fan."

Ebony chuckled. "Yeah, I heard."

Faith frowned at Cass. "You told her?"

"You quoting her song was too awesome not to mention. I'll be right back. Don't disappear on me," Cass said with a wink.

Faith smiled. "You're not getting rid of me that easy now."

"Good." Cass gave her a quick kiss before heading back out on stage.

She thanked all the artists that performed, talked about Pure Music artists with upcoming tours, and announced how much the event had raised so far for the Pure Music Children's Fund.

"The night is young, the liquor is free, and DJ Harmony is ready to get you all out on the dance floor so enjoy yourself everyone!" Cass said in closing before walking off the stage.

"Now, my fairy princess, I have something special for you." Cass took Faith's hand and led her from back stage.

Cass took her to the sundeck where a private table was set for dinner for two at the far end of the deck.

"What is this?" Faith asked as Cass pulled out one of the chairs for her to sit.

"It's our own private celebration," Cass said, grinning happily.

"You planned all of this? What if I had not shown up?"

"I would have been heartbroken and probably gifted this lovely private dinner to Ebony and Belinda in honor of their engagement," Cass said.

"Well, I'm happy for them but happier that I decided to attend," Faith said.

"So am I." Cass carefully leaned over the table to kiss her.

They were interrupted by someone clearing their throat.

"We'll finish this later," Cass said.

Faith smiled and looked to see who had interrupted their kiss and saw one of the "fox" servers holding a large satin pillow with her red shoes on them. Cass signaled for the server to come closer and took one of the shoes from the pillow. Butterflies fluttered in Faith's abdomen as Cass knelt in front of her, set the shoes down, lifted each foot to remove the shoes she wore, then slowly placed her red shoes on her feet, running her fingers along her ankles as she laced each shoe. When she finished, she lifted Faith's feet and placed a soft kiss on the exposed area of each foot. By the time she was done Faith's body was thrumming with excitement.

"Will you be my Cinderella?" she asked with a broad grin.

Faith leaned forward and cupped Cass's face in her hands. "Only if you promise to be my Prince Charming."

"Not even a fire breathing dragon could drag me away from you," Cass said.

Faith lowered her mouth to Cass's for a deeply sensual kiss that was rudely interrupted by cheering.

Faith looked past Cass to a small group of people watching them from halfway down the deck.

"What in the world?" Faith asked.

Cass lowered her head in embarrassment. "I'm sorry, you'll have to excuse my rude ass friends." She turned to look back at the group which consisted of Ebony and Belinda,

Chayse and Serena, Eve and Lynette, and Stephanie and Ezra, who to Faith's surprise had his arm around Stephanie's waist in a very familiar way. "Do you all mind?"

Laughing, they all turned and headed back to the main event area.

Cass turned back to Faith. "Now, where were we?"

"I believe my Prince Charming was pledging her undying devotion to me," Faith said with a mischievous grin.

Cass stood, pulling Faith up with her and into her arms where she pledged her love with a kiss that would make any princess fairy swoon.

About the Author

Anne Shade is an incurable romantic who believes there is no limit to love. She is dedicated to writing romances that show women who love women in a loving and positive light. She lives in West Orange, New Jersey, and when she is not writing about love she reads fantasy novels and helps make couples' wedding dreams a reality.

Books Available from Bold Strokes Books

Femme Tales by Anne Shade. Six women find themselves in their own real-life fairy tales when true love finds them in the most unexpected ways. (978-1-63555-657-5)

Jellicle Girl by Stevie Mikayne. One dark summer night, Beth and Jackie go out to the canoe dock. Two years later, Beth is still carrying the weight of what happened to Jackie. (978-1-63555-691-9)

Le Berceau by Julius Eks. If only Ben could tear his heart in two, then he wouldn't have to choose between the love of his life and the most beautiful boy he has ever seen. (978-1-63555-688-9)

My Date with a Wendigo by Genevieve McCluer. Elizabeth Rosseau finds her long lost love and the secret community of fiends she's now a part of. (978-1-63555-679-7)

On the Run by Charlotte Greene. Even when they're cute blondes, it's stupid to pick up hitchhikers, especially when they've just broken out of prison, but doing so is about to change Gwen's life forever. (978-1-63555-682-7)

Perfect Timing by Dena Blake. The choice between love and family has never been so difficult, and Lynn's and Maggie's different visions of the future may end their romance before it's begun. (978-1-63555-466-3)

The Mail Order Bride by R. Kent. When a mail order bride is thrust on Austin, he must choose between the bride he never wanted or the dream he lives for. (978-1-63555-678-0)

Through Love's Eyes by C.A. Popovich. When fate reunites Brittany Yardin and Amy Jansons, can they move beyond the pain of their past to find love? (978-1-63555-629-2)

To the Moon and Back by Melissa Brayden. Film actress Carly Daniel thinks that stage work is boring and unexciting, but when she accepts a lead role in a new play, stage manager Lauren Prescott tests both her heart and her ability to share the limelight. (978-1-63555-618-6)

Tokyo Love by Diana Jean. When Kathleen Schmitt is given the opportunity to be on the cutting edge of AI technology, she never thought a failed robotic love companion would bring her closer to her neighbor, Yuriko Velucci, and finding love in unexpected places. (978-1-63555-681-0)

Brooklyn Summer by Maggie Cummings. When opposites attract, can a summer of passion and adventure lead to a lifetime of love? (978-1-63555-578-3)

City Kitty and Country Mouse by Alyssa Linn Palmer. Pulled in two different directions, can a city kitty and country mouse fall in love and make it work? (978-1-63555-553-0)

Elimination by Jackie D. When a dangerous homegrown terrorist seeks refuge with the Russian mafia, the team will be put to the ultimate test. (978-1-63555-570-7)

In the Shadow of Darkness by Nicole Stiling. Angeline Vallencourt is a reluctant vampire who must decide what she wants more—obscurity, revenge, or the woman who makes her feel alive. (978-1-63555-624-7)

On Second Thought by C. Spencer. Madisen is falling hard for Rae. Even single life and co-parenting are beginning to click. At least, that is, until her ex-wife begins to have second thoughts. (978-1-63555-415-1)

Out of Practice by Carsen Taite. When attorney Abby Keane discovers the wedding blogger tormenting her client is the woman she had a passionate, anonymous vacation fling with, sparks and subpoenas fly. Legal Affairs: one law firm, three best friends, three chances to fall in love. (978-1-63555-359-8)

Providence by Leigh Hays. With every click of the shutter, photographer Rebekiah Kearns finds it harder and harder to keep Lindsey Blackwell in focus without getting too close. (978-1-63555-620-9)

Taking a Shot at Love by KC Richardson. When academic and athletic worlds collide, will English professor Celeste Bouchard and basketball coach Lisa Tobias ignore their attraction to achieve their professional goals? (978-1-63555-549-3)

Flight to the Horizon by Julie Tizard. Airline captain Kerri Sullivan and flight attendant Janine Case struggle to survive an emergency water landing and overcome dark secrets to give love a chance to fly. (978-1-63555-331-4)

In Helen's Hands by Nanisi Barrett D'Arnuk. As her mistress, Helen pushes Mickey to her sensual limits, delivering the pleasure only a BDSM lifestyle can provide her. (978-1-63555-639-1)

Jamis Bachman, Ghost Hunter by Jen Jensen. In Sage Creek, Utah, a poltergeist stirs to life and past secrets emerge. (978-1-63555-605-6)

Moon Shadow by Suzie Clarke. Add betrayal, season with survival, then serve revenge smokin' hot with a sharp knife. (978-1-63555-584-4)

Spellbound by Jean Copeland and Jackie D. When the supernatural worlds of good and evil face off, love might be what saves them all. (978-1-63555-564-6)

Temptation by Kris Bryant. Can experienced nanny Cassie Miller deny her growing attraction and keep her relationship with her boss professional? Or will they sidestep propriety and give in to temptation? (978-1-63555-508-0)

The Inheritance by Ali Vali. Family ties bring Tucker Delacroix and Willow Vernon together, but they could also tear them, and any chance they have at love, apart. (978-1-63555-303-1)

Thief of the Heart by MJ Williamz. Kit Hanson makes a living seducing rich women in casinos and relieving them of the expensive jewelry most won't even miss. But her streak ends when she meets beautiful FBI agent Savannah Brown. (978-1-63555-572-1)

Date Night by Raven Sky. Quinn and Riley are celebrating their one-year anniversary. Such an important milestone is bound to result in some extraordinary sexual adventures, but precisely how extraordinary is up to you, dear reader. (978-1-63555-655-1)

Face Off by PJ Trebelhorn. Hockey player Savannah Wells rarely spends more than a night with any one woman, but when photographer Madison Scott buys the house next door, she's forced to rethink what she expects out of life. (978-1-63555-480-9)

Hot Ice by Aurora Rey, Elle Spencer, Erin Zak. Can falling in love melt the hearts of the iciest ice queens? Join Aurora Rey, Elle Spencer, and Erin Zak to find out! (978-1-63555-513-4)

Line of Duty by VK Powell. Dr. Dylan Carlyle's professional and personal life is turned upside down when a tragic event at Fairview Station pits her against ambitious, handsome police officer Finley Masters. (978-1-63555-486-1)

London Undone by Nan Higgins. London Craft reinvents her life after reading a childhood letter to her future self and in doing so finds the love she truly wants. (978-1-63555-562-2)

Lunar Eclipse by Gun Brooke. Moon De Cruz lives alone on an uninhabited planet after being shipwrecked in space. Her life changes forever when Captain Beaux Lestarion's arrival threatens the planet and Moon's freedom. (978-1-63555-460-1)

One Small Step by Michelle Binfield. Iris and Cam discover the meaning of taking chances and following your heart, even if it means getting hurt. (978-1-63555-596-7)

Shadows of a Dream by Nicole Disney. Rainn has the talent to take her rock band all the way, but falling in love is a powerful distraction, and her new girlfriend's meth addiction might just take them both down. (978-1-63555-598-1)

Someone to Love by Jenny Frame. When Davina Trent is given an unexpected family, can she let nanny Wendy Darling teach her to open her heart to the children and to Wendy? (978-1-63555-468-7)

Tinsel by Kris Bryant. Did a sweet kitten show up to help Jessica Raymond and Taylor Mitchell find each other? Or is the holiday spirit to blame for their special connection? (978-1-63555-641-4)

Uncharted by Robyn Nyx. As Rayne Marcellus and Chase Stinsen track the legendary Golden Trinity, they must learn to put their differences aside and depend on one another to survive. (978-1-63555-325-3)

Where We Are by Annie McDonald. Can two women discover a way to walk on the same path together and discover the gift of staying in one spot, in time, in space, and in love? (978-1-63555-581-3)

A Moment in Time by Lisa Moreau. A longstanding family feud separates two women who unexpectedly fall in love at an antique clock shop in a small Louisiana town. (978-1-63555-419-9)

Aspen in Moonlight by Kelly Wacker. When art historian Melissa Warren meets Sula Johansen, director of a local bear conservancy, she discovers that love can come in unexpected and unusual forms. (978-1-63555-470-0)

Back to September by Melissa Brayden. Small bookshop owner Hannah Shepard and famous romance novelist Parker Bristow maneuver the landscape of their two very different worlds to find out if love can win out in the end. (978-1-63555-576-9)

Changing Course by Brey Willows. When the woman of your dreams falls from the sky, you'd better be ready to catch her. (978-1-63555-335-2)

Cost of Honor by Radclyffe. First Daughter Blair Powell and Homeland Security Director Cameron Roberts face adversity when their enemies stop at nothing to prevent President Andrew Powell's reelection. (978-1-63555-582-0)

Fearless by Tina Michele. Determined to overcome her debilitating fear through exposure therapy, Laura Carter all but fails before she's even begun until dolphin trainer Jillian Marshall dedicates herself to helping Laura defeat the nightmares of her past. (978-1-63555-495-3)

Not Dead Enough by J.M. Redmann. A woman who may or may not be dead drags Micky Knight into a messy con game. (978-1-63555-543-1)

Not Since You by Fiona Riley. When Charlotte boards her honeymoon cruise single and comes face-to-face with Lexi, the high school love she left behind, she questions every decision she has ever made. (978-1-63555-474-8)

Not Your Average Love Spell by Barbara Ann Wright. Four women struggle with who to love and who to hate while fighting to rid a kingdom of an evil invading force. (978-1-63555-327-7)

Tennessee Whiskey by Donna K. Ford. Dane Foster wants to put her life on pause and ask for a redo, a chance for something that matters. Emma Reynolds is that chance. (978-1-63555-556-1)